AT FIRST SIGHT

Byroney was on the back stoop, washing her face before breakfast, when she felt eyes upon her.

"Howdy." The man stood a trifle over six feet, dressed in deerskins. His flat-brimmed hat sat squarely on his raven-black hair. Around his waist was a broad sash with a belt ax and scabbard knife. A shotbag and powderhorn were slung over his left shoulder. His large brown hands rested easily on the barrel of his grounded long rifle. Byroney looked up and directly into the strangest eyes she'd ever seen . . . a piercing grey-blue.

The air between them seemed to snap and pop like a pine-log fire.

AMERICAN DREAMS

The
Innkeeper's
Daughter

LOU KASSEM

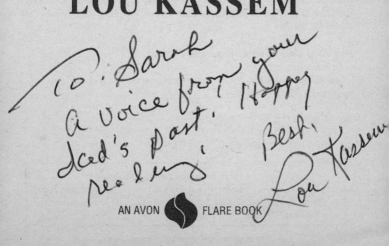

To: Sarah
A voice from your
dad's past. Happy
reading.
Best,
Lou Kassem

AN AVON FLARE BOOK

THE INNKEEPER'S DAUGHTER is an original publication of Avon Books. This work has never before appeared in book form.

AVON BOOKS
A division of
The Hearst Corporation
1350 Avenue of the Americas
New York, New York 10019

Copyright © 1996 by Lou Kassem
Excerpt from *Reyna's Reward* copyright © 1996 by Wanda Dionne
Published by arrangement with the author
Library of Congress Catalog Card Number: 96-96082
ISBN: 0-380-78348-7
RL: 6.8

First Avon Flare Printing: September 1996

AVON FLARE TRADEMARK REG. U.S. PAT. OFF. AND IN OTHER COUNTRIES, MARCA REGISTRADA, HECHO EN U.S.A.

Printed in the U.S.A.

RA   10   9   8   7   6   5   4   3   2   1

For those who follow their hearts
and fight for their dreams

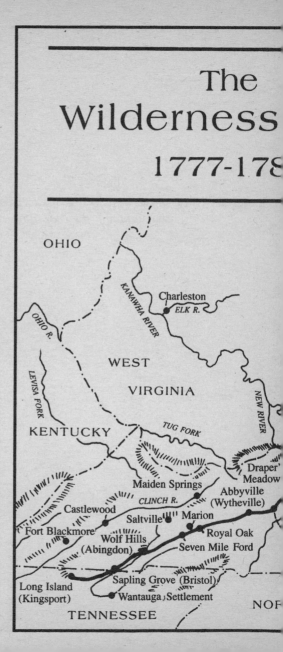

The
Wilderness
1777-178

OHIO

OHIO R.

KANAWHA RIVER

Charleston
ELK R.

LEVISA FORK

WEST

VIRGINIA

NEW RIVER

KENTUCKY

TUG FORK

Draper'
Meadow

Maiden Springs

Abbyville
(Wytheville)

CLINCH R.

Castlewood

Saltville

Marion

Fort Blackmore

Wolf Hills
(Abingdon)

Royal Oak

Seven Mile Ford

Long Island
(Kingsport)

Sapling Grove (Bristol)

Wantauga Settlement

NOF

TENNESSEE

Road

POTOMAC RIVER

Wadkin's
Ferry
Martinsburg
Winchester

Strasburg

SHENANDOAH RIVER

Harrisonburg

Swift Run
Gap

SHENANDOAH MTS.

Staunton
(Orverly)

Rockfish
Gap

ALLEGHENY MTS.

Lexington

Natural Bridge

BLUE RIDGE MTS.

APPALACHIAN MTS.

JAMES RIVER

Buchanan

Salem

es Ferry
dford)

Big Lick
(Roanoke)

ROANOKE RIVER

Christianburg

hiswell

n

VIRGINIA

Map by Virginia Norey

CAROLINA

Chapter 1

"You'll be sorry you left, Byroney Frazer!" Amelia Burke screeched from the upstairs balcony. "The wild Indians will get you! You'll be sorry."

Byroney did not look back or wave. Eyes straight ahead, she sat beside her mother and brother in the open wagon seat. Her father and oldest brother Andrew rode alongside. Irrepressible, seven-year-old Nathaniel bounded back and forth in the wagon bed, waving and shouting good-bye to everyone.

Colin clucked to the horses, and they moved away from Burkeslea Hall.

"I hope you get scalped!" was Amelia's fading cry.

"Amelia's such an unmannerly bairn," remarked Mrs. Frazer, her patrician face stern. "I foresee trouble for that lass."

"Trouble?" By said with an indignant snort. "I don't think wild Indians could have worse tantrums." A slight smile curved her full lips. "I do believe this is the first time Miss Amelia didn't get exactly what she wanted."

"Makes me glad I worked outside with Pa," Colin said. "How'd you put up with that banshee?"

Byroney shrugged. "Being a companion to Miss Amelia was my task. 'Tis finished." The words were hardly out of her mouth when she saw a figure by the iron gates. Was it *not* finished? Would the squire find a reason to keep them?

Squire Burke, mounted on a handsome stallion, waited at the end of the lane. "Good fortune to you and your family, Ian," he said, tipping his tricorn hat to the ladies. "You've served me well."

A small sigh of relief escaped from Byroney's lips. "Value given for value received, Squire," Ian answered.

"Wish you'd reconsider and stay on. 'Tis a dangerous venture you've set upon."

Ian Frazer's jaw stiffened. "Many thanks, Squire. But we're stubborn, we Scots. We have a plan, and, dangerous or not, we'll keep to it."

Squire Burke nodded, making his jowls quiver. "So be it. The Crown needs support on the frontier, eh? Mistress Burke will miss your fine needle, Margaret. And I know Amelia will miss your company, Byroney."

"Thank you, Squire," Margaret Frazer said graciously.

Byroney merely smiled. The Crown would find no support in these Highland hearts! Her father was a great admirer of Thomas Jefferson and the fiery orator Patrick Henry, though he was careful where he said so.

"Farewell then." With a flourish, the squire cantered away, his well-padded rump bouncing in the saddle.

Colin slapped the reins, and the horses moved off.

As soon as they reached the main road and were off Burke land, Andrew stood in his stirrups, waved his hat, and yelled, "The Frazers are free!"

"Three cheers for freedom!" responded Colin.

Ragged, happy cheers broke from every throat. Byroney's hip-hip-hurrah was loudest of all. Even with a kind master such as Squire Burke, being owned was

2

being owned! Amelia nad never let her forget her position.

"We made a canny deal," Ian Frazer said happily. Then, looking hopefully at his family, said, " 'Twas not so terrible, was it?"

"No," Margaret answered quickly, "but our hearts are lighter now."

"So are your petticoats, I'll wager," Byroney's father said, eyes twinkling.

That brought laughter from everyone. Except Nat. He'd been too young to share the secret of Mama's petticoats.

"Why are you laughing? What's so funny?" he demanded.

"Tell Nat the story, Papa," Byroney urged.

"Please, Pa," begged Nat.

"Weel now, I suppose a story would help ease our journey. Mind us o' how we came to be traveling this road," Ian said.

Nat squirmed into a comfortable position among their belongings. "Go on, Pa."

Ian Frazer cleared his throat, looking off into the distance. "Scotland was a proud and independent country . . . until we came under the heel o' the British Crown. The Lowland Scots took fairly well to English rule. Not so with us Highlanders. The Crown took measures to crush our independent spirit—much as King George is doing here in the Colonies. We resisted. After we were defeated at Colloden, one vengeful law followed another. Our lairds were cash poor and commenced to sell their land. Scots by the thousands were cleared from their ancestral homes in those Highland Clearances."

Her father's Scottish burr grew thicker as he talked. It brought with it the smell of heather and the feel of a Highland wind sweeping through the glens. Byroney

3

sighed. There was no heather or crisp wind in these hot, sandy flatlands.

Ian Frazer continued. "Yer mither and me saw the way the wind was blowin'. We knew we must take our bairns and go from Glen Ellyn. The Colonies held promise, but if we paid our passage, we'd have naught left for starting afresh. Then, as luck would have it, I went doon to Edinburgh with the laird and met up with Squire Burke. Happens he's searching for an overseer for his plantation in the Virginia Colony! Laird Frazer gave me a boosting. And I hied meself back to Glen Ellyn to talk wi' yer ma and yer Uncle Duncan. 'Tis how we came to be redemptioners, pledging ourselves to three years o' service for passage to Virginia. Duncan, as planned, paid his passage and scouted land for us."

"I know that story," Nat said impatiently. "What about Ma's petticoats?"

Ian laughed. "I'm coming to 'em. Saved the best for last. 'Twas your Ma's idea. We converted all our worldly goods into gold sovereigns and sewed the coins into pockets in her petticoat! And tha's why we have the wherewithal to begin our new life."

"Three cheers for Ma!" yelled Nat.

Margaret Frazer's face colored as they cheered her shrewdness. "Go on, you rowdies! 'Twas mere common sense."

"We'll need a heap o' that in the comin' months, Maggie luv," Ian said. "Quick up those horses, Colin. We've Angus McKay's to reach before nightfall."

Byroney scrambled into the wagon bed to give her mother more room and to keep rambunctious Nat amused.

Nat cosied beside her. "You think ole Prissy-mouth Amelia was right? Will we have to fight off Indians?"

"Uncle Duncan says there's peace with the Cherokee

right now. Just in case the peace don't hold, they've built a fort at Wolf Hills."

Nat's face crumpled. "I wanted to see Indians! I bet there's no wolves at Wolf Hills either."

"Don't fash yourself, Nat. I expect the frontier's still wild enough for the both of us."

"Tell me a frontier story, By."

"Shall I tell you Uncle Duncan's tale of how Wolf Hills got its name?"

"Oh, yes, do!"

Blessed with the Gaelic gift of storytelling, Byroney launched into the tale of Daniel Boone's famed battle with a cave of wolves. She told it even better than her uncle had on his last visit.

Freed at last from the confines of being Mistress Amelia's dogsbody, By's imagination took flight. She added adventures with bears, mountain lions, and even banshees.

"Mind how you go, Byroney," cautioned her mother, looking back at Nat's wide-eyed stare. "You'll scare the lad out o' ten year growth."

"No, she won't, Ma. I know 'tis only By's tall tale telling."

Colin looked over his shoulder, grinning wolfishly. "Mayhap her tales are not s' tall."

"Colin!"

"Sorry, Ma. But Uncle Duncan warned us o' the hardships we face. Won't be all berries and cream on the frontier."

"My tongue's tired anyways," By said. She nestled deeper into her nook and pulled her bonnet down over her eyes. "I'm for a nap."

She had no intention of sleeping away her first few hours of freedom. She wished to savor it. Sometimes she'd thought this day would never come. For three whole years she'd been at Amelia's beck and call, a virtual slave to her every whim. Hard as it was, she'd matched her mother's calm and never complained. A bargain was a bargain. Frazers kept their word. Now she was her own master. Could do as she pleased. Lordy, freedom felt good! Even the air was sweeter.

At noon they stopped to rest the horses, stretch their own legs, and fill their stomachs. Andrew and Colin changed places. But no amount of pleading would get Byroney a turn on horseback.

"You've ridden aught but a pony, lass," her father said kindly.

"I can ride well, Papa. Old George, the groom, said I had a natural seat. Made Amelia plumb furious."

"Old George liked to please you. As I do," her father replied. "There'll be time enough once we're on our way. I don't wish to start out with broken bones."

Knowing her father hated to deny her anything, By nodded. "All right, Papa. But do you promise I can ride soon?"

"I promise. And, if all goes well with our venture, you may have a horse all your own one day."

"Me, too, Pa?"

"You, also, Nathaniel."

"Don't count your chickens, Ian."

"Why not, Maggie luv? Once we send the English scuttling back to their proper place, the West will open like a flower in spring. And we Frazers will be there offering a place of comfort on the Wilderness Road."

Margaret bounced on the hard seat as they hit a rut. "First we must get there!"

In the late afternoon they arrived at McKay Station. Angus and his wife Nora came out to meet them. After hugs and greetings were exchanged, Angus said, "Yer wagon's 'round back, Ian. Unload your belongings on it and drive it over to the south meadow with the others. I'll see this wagon gets back to Squire Burke."

6

"We're beholden, Angus."

"And I'll collect," the little Scotsman promised, his eyes twinkling. "Settle in with Sam Cutter and come back to sup with us."

"Aye. Thank ye kindly. 'Twill be good to hear the mither tongue," Ian said.

The new wagon was longer, narrower, and covered with a canvas top. It was already filled with the supplies Ian and Duncan had ordered. The Frazers made short work of packing their few belongings inside.

The dray horses, Bonnie and Donald, were none too sure about the new contraption. But with Ian's gentle urging they finally pulled together and off went the Frazers to join the other travelers.

"Look! The wagons look like ships!" By cried, as the other wagons came into view.

A lone horseman rode out to meet them. "Howdy. You be the Frazers?"

"Aye."

"Sam Cutter." He raised his wide-brimmed hat to the women. "I'm t' lead you through. Pick a spot and settle in. I'll check by later."

While Colin and Andrew unhitched the horses and took them downstream to pasture, By and Nat went upstream to fetch water from the bubbly creek.

"Don't linger," warned Mrs. Frazer. "We need to wash up and be to the McKays' for supper."

Byroney would have preferred to stay with the wagons and meet the other adventurers, but one did not refuse Scottish hospitality.

Sam Cutter returned just as they were leaving. A smile twinkled in his eyes as he checked them off a list. "The Frazers: Ian and Margaret, a pair o' strapping lads, a tad, and a curly redheaded gel o' marriageable age."

7

"I'm not a redhead and I'm not marriageable!" By sputtered, her blue eyes flashing a cold fire.

"Make that one lass with spirit," Sam said, grinning wickedly. "Duncan said that'd set you off."

"I'll get Uncle Duncan for that," By muttered. "I'll get him good!"

"Now, Byroney Rose, you ken what a cutup your uncle is," her mother said. "That man would tease a tree stump."

"Those two are redheads," By stormed, pointing to her grinning sixteen- and seventeen-year-old brothers. "My hair is rusty brown like yours. And, fourteen or no, I'll not be wedding anyone anytime soon. I just got my freedom!"

"You're right," Andrew said solemnly. "Who would want to wed a Briary Rose?"

Colin and Nat roared with laughter.

"Briary Rose! Briary Rose!" chanted Nat, holding his sides.

Margaret Frazer quelled them with a look. "Let's be on to supper," she said, herding her sons in front of her.

"You're not fourteen yet," Nat piped, firing one last shot.

Red-faced, Byroney started after them.

"Gals do marry young out hyar," Sam Cutter said apologetically.

"Some girls may. Not me. I'm particular," By snapped.

"Well, I allus heered it was the prize rose what had the sharpest thorns," Sam said. "Reckon I heered right?"

Byroney flashed him a smile. "I'm named for my granny's own prize rose. One plucked them wi' great caution."

"I'll pass th' word," Sam promised, laughing. "Me? I'd say you was well named." He turned to Ian. "We

8

pull out at first light. Yer brother's a'waitin'. None too patiently, I'm afeered.''

"We'll be ready, Sam. We're eager, too,'' Ian said.

For Byroney that was an understatement.

Chapter 2

The wagon jolted—swayed—slid backward—and finally came to a standstill.

By scrambled up and poked her head through the front flap. For a moment she couldn't see . . . the world was a blur of white. Wind howled through Rockfish Gap like the Hag of Loch Dhu. Andrew and her pa were whitened stumps on the wagon seat. "What happened?" she screamed into the wind.

". . . inside! Hold on!" her father ordered.

The wagon jerked forward, throwing her head over teakettle.

"What happened?" Colin asked.

"I don't know. Couldn't see past the horses' ears."

"Are we almost over?" asked Nat, voice aquiver.

"I couldn't tell," By answered, crawling under the blankets.

They'd been caught by a blinding spring snowstorm halfway over the high, blue ridge of mountains separating them from the Wilderness Road. Stuck on the narrow track and fearing rockslides, the settlers had no choice but to drive their teams onward. By was glad she could no longer see the sheer drop on their left.

"Don't fash yourself, Nathaniel. Pa will get us to safety," Margaret Frazer said with calm assurance.

"We're starting down!" Colin cried as the wagon dipped forward.

Even over the howling wind they could hear the protesting screech of the wagon brake. Going down was more dangerous than going up. Though Sam had spaced them out, they could overrun the wagon in front or be hit by the wagon behind. Either way spelled disaster.

"Start us a tune, Byroney," her mother requested. " 'Twill help pass the time."

Sing? She could hardly swallow for the lump in her throat! Nevertheless, she began "The Jolly Juggler."

Her mother's clear alto joined in perfect harmony. Eventually, Colin and Nat chimed in.

The juggler had thirty improbable items in the air when By heard Sam Cutter cry, "Circle up!"

"The Lord be thanked!" Margaret Frazer said.

"Amen!"

As soon as the wagon halted they all piled out, glad to have their feet on solid ground once more.

Sam had found a sheltered cove and Cam, his freight driver, had built a roaring fire. Through the swirling snow, By counted three other wagons besides Sam's . . . Tyler's, Hoge's, and Price's. Six yet to come!

After only five days she knew every wagon and every man, woman, and child in them. Like her granny's Surprise Stew, they were interesting bits of everything from everywhere. Best of all, she'd found two new friends, Lydie Wilson and Charity McIver. Would their wagons make it?

"Come in out of the weather," her ma urged. "We can watch from here."

Reluctantly, By went back inside.

Long minutes passed before the next wagon came. Then, one by one, four others rumbled in.

More time passed. The tenth wagon did not appear.

"Who's missing, By?" asked Nat.

"The Wilsons. They should have come by now."

"Look! Sam's riding out to check on 'em," Nat cried.

The camp grew strangely quiet after Sam left. Folks went about their business with one ear cocked . . . including Byroney.

When the tenth wagon finally came into view a wild cheer went up. By felt ten pounds lighter.

Later, Sam poked his head through the canvas flap of the Frazer wagon. "Cob's got Settler Stew ready. Come, eat."

The Frazers grabbed bowls and spoons and hurried to the fire.

Despite the cold, the mood was festive. Shared danger had drawn everyone together like family. Lydie, Charity, and By hugged like long-lost sisters.

"I thought we were goners when our wheels went over," Lydie said. "I said my prayers and prepared to die."

"We prayed *all* the way down," Charity said.

"We sang," By said, laughing.

"Sang?" both girls said in unison.

"Making a joyful noise unto the Lord, I suppose. Wasn't pretty, but it kept us from screaming."

"Once we get to Beverly, I'm not setting foot ever again in *any* wagon," Lydie declared.

Charity nodded. "I've a mind to walk all the way to the Watauga Settlement."

By was sorely tired of riding in the bumpity wagon herself. Trudging alongside wasn't much better. If only there were a spare horse . . .

"It's your turn, By. Hold out your bowl," prompted Charity.

Byroney complied.

12

While others hurried back to their wagons with the fragrant stew, By lingered by the fire. An idea had popped into her head. "Mr. Cutter?"

"Told ya to call me Sam, didn't I?"

"Sam, then. Why'd you have that paint horse hitched behind your wagon?"

"Buck? Just in case ole Sly throws a shoe or sumpin. Buck, he don't like it none too much."

Hiding a smile and her hopes, By said, "Reckon Buck would rather be out front, eh?" She'd quickly adopted the speech and manner of the frontiersman.

"Aye-ya. Never been a follower, has Buck."

By pulled a long face. "Sure hate to see any animal unhappy. Reckon I could help out and ride Buck some?"

Sam, dressed from head to toe in fringed buckskins and not seeming to feel the cold at all, threw back his head and laughed. "Reckon not, Missy. Though I sure 'preciate your concern. Buck come by his name natural, summat like you. 'Sides, he don't cotton to females one little bit."

"Oh," By said, trying to hide her disappointment. "Could I try to make friends with Buck, Sam? When we get to the Shenandoah Valley, I mean?"

"No harm in tryin'. You a rider, are ye?" Sam asked, giving her a hard squint.

"I have a very good seat," By answered confidently.

"You'd need it with Buck. He hates anything in skirts. Now scoot on back to yer wagon 'fore you turn to a icicle."

Mind churning, By obeyed. There was more than one way to skin a cat—or get a horse. Somehow she'd make ole Buck a friend!

"Shut that flap," Andrew ordered when she crawled into the wagon. Peering closely at her, he said, "What are you up to now, By?"

13

"Nothing. Why?"

"Your eyes are dancing a Highland fling. 'Tis not from the cold, I'll wager."

"Mind your own business, Andrew. Would you like a story, Nat?"

"Yes!"

Byroney hid her excitement by telling old Scottish tales. She even made up a few of her own.

Though they pretended to sleep, By could tell Andrew and Colin listened, too.

Two days later the settlement of Beverly came into view. The spring snow had melted almost as quickly as it had fallen. The lush valley of rolling, greening fields spread invitingly between the two mountain ranges. Small burns sparkled and gushed in ample abundance throughout the famed Shenandoah Valley.

Water, however good for future crops, left the dirt track a slushy, mushy mess for the loaded wagons to plow through.

Lydie, Charity, and By picked their way through the mire ahead of the lumbering wagons.

"'Tis good farm land," said Lydie Wilson. "Pa will be plowing his fields and planting his crops in his head. By the time we reach Beverly he'll have every inch spoken for."

"I wish you weren't leaving us here," Charity McIver said. "We just became friends. Beverly doesn't look very big or important."

"It will be. It's Augusta's county seat," Lydie replied. "Bet it's bigger than where you're headed."

Before either girl could reply, a group of boys galloped past them, flinging mud in all directions.

"Boys!" Charity yelled, shaking her fists at the riders. "They think they're so smart!"

By brushed mud from her skirts. Seeing the carefree

14

boys go by gave her an idea. "Let's find a store first thing," she said. "I need to buy me something."

"What?" asked Charity and Lydie in unison.

Byroney grinned. "You'll see."

Beverly wasn't a very large settlement. Finding a general store was easy. By made her purchase with the money her Pa had given her her last birthday and went to say good-bye to Lydie.

"What do you want with a big, floppy man's hat?" asked Charity.

"Is it a present for your Pa?"

"Nope. It's for me. I don't aim to ride that wagon or go shank's mare all the way to Wolf Hills."

"What's a hat got to do with it?" Charity asked, frowning.

"You'll see."

"Reckon I won't," Lydie said, giving both girls a hug. "Papa's gonna leave without me if I don't hurry." With a wave, she raced after her father's wagon.

Charity and By made their way back to the wagons, with Charity pestering every step of the way.

"Charity, for over ten years I was like that bird circling up yonder: free to be me. Then for three years I had to be somebody I wasn't. Mind you, it was for a good cause. But I don't aim to let it happen again. I'm not gonna miss a second o' this journey west." And despite Charity's still-puzzled look, that's all she would say on the matter.

Charity flounced off to her wagon without another word.

Wishing to make up for lost time and take advantage of the good weather, Sam led the wagons out of Beverly at first light. At last, they were traveling the Wilderness Road. Though by most standards, it could hardly be called a road. Except near the scattered settlements, the road was mere wagon ruts, full of potholes and jutting stones.

By waited until the second day out to put her plan into action. While everyone else was finishing breakfast she slipped inside the wagon and put on a pair of Colin's breeches and a linsey-woolsey shirt. Quickly, she tucked her thick auburn hair under the big hat and slipped out. She hoped anyone who saw her would mistake her for Colin as she slaunched back to Sam's wagon. "Mornin', Cob. Sam forget t' tell you to saddle Buck?"

Cob's weather-crinkled blue eyes raked her over—twice. "Reckon so. You aim to ride Buck today?"

"Aye."

Cob silently got out a blanket and saddle and threw them over Buck's back. The bridle followed. "He's all yourn."

Buck stood placidly.

Heart pounding, By took the reins, put her foot in the stirrup, and bounced aboard with a plop. *Easy as pie,* she thought, as Buck took a few slow steps.

The next instant she was flying through the air.

Buck was calmly munching a patch of grass when her vision cleared.

"You hurt?"

Without turning, By got to her feet. She seemed to be all of a piece. "Nay." Picking up her hat, she stuffed her hair back inside before she turned to face Sam and Cob. "Me and Buck were just gettin' acquainted." Head high, she marched over, grabbed the dangling reins, and remounted.

Sam strode up, putting a hand on the bridle. "You sure, Missy?"

Byroney nodded.

Sam let go.

Buck threw her again.

Slowly, By picked herself out of the dirt and, with a determined fire in her eyes, remounted.

"Shorten yer reins and use yer legs," Sam called.

Sunfishing and whirligigging, Buck threw her twice more before settling down to an easy walk.

Sam watched her for a few minutes. "Reckon you do have a good seat in th' saddle, Missy."

"Yes, when I manage to stay in saddle I do," By answered, trying to smile. "He's a mite frisky."

"You stuck like a cocklebur," Cob said. "You're apt to feel it come tomorrow."

"You mean it gets worse?" By asked. She already ached something fierce.

"It does," Sam assured her. "Might as well ride Buck whilst you can move though."

"Thanks, Sam." Back straight, she followed Sam toward the line of wagons. Sore or not, her plan was working!

Margaret Frazer was not pleased. "Byroney Rose, just look at you! Whatever do you think you're doing? Get down this instant!"

"Leave her be, Maggie," Ian said, chuckling. " 'Pears to me she's earned her mount."

"She's in breeches!"

"Breeches don't make a man. 'Twill do her no harm."

"You stole my clothes," Colin said when he saw her.

"Borrowed," By corrected. "Buck doesn't like females. I had to fool him. Besides, I only took your outgrown ones."

"You are responsible for the washing and mending," her mother said sternly. "I'll no have you in filthy rags."

"Yes, Mama."

"Let's see if you can really ride," Andrew challenged. "Race you to the head o' the column."

Byroney kicked Buck into a gallop and held on for dear life.

That night bandy-legged Cob stopped by their wagon, carrying a steaming cup of liquid that he thrust at By. "Hyar, drink this. Hit'll ease you summat."

"What is it?"

"A tisane made from willow bark. I allus carry some."

"Every inch o' me hurts," By confessed. "I'm obliged, Cob."

With a knowing nod, Cob warned, "Hit's a soother, not a cure."

By found what he meant the next morning when she tried to get up. But as soon as the soreness wore off, she was back on Buck. And despite some raised eyebrows at her scandalous attire, she rode almost every day.

The taste of freedom was addictive. The more By had, the more she wanted. Little by little, as they wound over hill and dale, she accquired more—riding out with her pa to hunt, tracking game, and even learning to load and shoot. At first, some of the men were uncomfortable when she tagged along. But Sam encouraged her, saying all the women should learn some of these skills.

"It isn't fitting, Ian," her mother whispered one night after they'd all bedded down. "Byroney is your *daughter*. She has no business riding and hunting like your sons."

"Does she neglect her woman's duties, Maggie luv?"

"Nay. She does her share and more."

"Then where's the harm?"

"Ian, it doesn't seem proper!"

"Maggie, things are different on the frontier. Sam wants to teach all the women to load and shoot. Byroney will be tied to hearth and home soon enough. She'll settle in once we get to Wolf Hills."

"I hope you are right, Ian. I would not have her hurt by this wild streak."

"Nor would I. But have you noticed how our Byroney Rose has blossomed since we left Burkeslea? She's a bonny, happy lass again. Minds me more o' you every day."

"Mayhap she does favor me," Margaret conceded, "but she has the wild Frazer fire burning inside her."

Ian chuckled. "That's no so terrible, is it, luv?"

Byroney burrowed under the covers. She shouldn't be listening to this private conversation! Yet how could she help it in this cramped wagon? Still, she'd learned something. She'd better go carefully.

For the next few days she did more than her share of the chores. She even took an extra turn minding the little ones. Telling onc talc aftcr anothcr, shc had the children following her as if she were the Pied Piper.

"Where do you get these stories?" Charity asked, huffing alongside her.

"Some from books. Some my granny told me. Some are true, and some I make up in my head."

"Which was the Witch o' the Mountains? It wasn't true, was it?" Charity asked, shivering as she looked at the mountains closing in around them.

"It was out of my head, silly goose. Not a word o' truth in it."

"Well, I wager no child will wander far this night!"

"That's why I told it," By replied. "Sam said some of the boys were going off into the woods after we made camp."

"I wish you'd help with the younguns every day," Charity said wistfully. "They're so good for you." She had four active little brothers and sisters to mind.

"Don't even think of it! I just did the extra to please Ma. I'm off on the hunt tomorrow."

"Reckon I'd starve to death if I had to shoot my supper. Me and the other women keep putting off Sam Cutter's gun lessons."

"You all better learn. Out here you might need it," warned By.

Byroney's warning proved true, if not her brag about going on the hunt. The hunters were going on foot, and her father refused to let her traipse along. "You'd hold us back, By. Your legs are not up to mountain hiking."

The hunting party had already left when a huge black bear lumbered from the nearby woods and, in the blink of an eye, snatched the swaddled Johnson baby in its jaws.

Screeching, Mrs. Johnson attacked the bear with an iron skillet.

The bear swatted her against the wagon like an annoying fly.

Lucinda Gillis, ignoring the gun propped by her wagon, grabbed a smoldering log from the fire and charged the bear.

The bear dropped the baby and fled.

When the dust was settled, miraculously, no one was seriouly hurt. Baby Jamie had a knot on his noggin and Mrs. Gillis had scorched hands.

The hunting party, hearing shouting, returned dragging the bear that had run right at them.

"No need to hunt for our supper now," Sam said. "This mama bear's winter lean but still good eatin'."

Lucinda Gillis stepped up, holding her red hands gingerly. "Soon as these are mended, I'd be proud if you'd learn me 'bout shooting a gun, Mr. Cutter."

A murmur of agreement came from the other women.

Sam smiled. "I'd be proud t' learn you. Mayhap Miz Johnson would give us all skillet lessons, too."

"I'd be proud to," Mrs. Johnson said. "My mama said this skillet would come in handy could I figure out how to use it. Reckon I just did."

Laughter eased the tension, and the wagons got under way.

Slowly but surely, the wagons plodded along, up and over mountains, fording creeks, and ferrying over rivers. Except for regularly getting stuck in the mud, breaking wheels, and constantly having to reshoe horses, the group proceeded at a pace that satisfied Sam.

"This here's the squeeze-end o' the Shenandoah Valley, By," Sam said as they approached Big Lick. "From here on it gets a mite hilly. Purdiest country they is."

She had to agree. Though the Wilderness Road narrowed considerably as it wound through the greening mountains, the scenery was music to her mountain-born soul. She'd never felt more alive. "They're not Scotland's mountains, Sam. But somehow I feel like I'm coming home."

"Mountains get in yer blood, that's fer sartin," Sam replied.

The mountains felt like home to others, too. Before the wagons crossed the New River at Ingles Ferry, the Price and Hoge wagons dropped out. "Looks a fair place to settle," Emmet Price said. "Me and the Hoges will mosey upriver a ways and look fer a spot."

Seven wagons moved on to Fort Chiswell and Abbyville. Fewer and fewer homesteads were seen. The Great Road, as some called it, was not deserted. Farmers, walkers, and men on horseback hailed the travelers regularly.

"Mr. Cutter says we'll make Wolf Hills tomorrow," Charity said sorrowfully. "I'll miss you, By. Wish you was going on to the Watauga Settlement."

"I'll miss you, too. Maybe you'll come stay at our inn someday."

"Or maybe you'll visit our mill."

"Would you welcome me, breeches and all?" By teased.

"You'd be welcome if you rode up buck naked, Byroney Frazer!"

"Keep the latch out then. The innkeeper's daughter may pay a visit to the miller's daughter one day," By said, laughing.

"Promise?"

"I promise I'll try. You, too?"

"Me, too."

The next afternoon an imposing figure, riding a big sorrel horse, approached the wagons at full gallop. "Halloo, wagons!" the man yelled, waving his hat.

"Mama!" By shouted, seeing the blaze of red hair. "Uncle Duncan's come to meet us. We're here!"

Chapter 3

"'Tis a wonder, Duncan!" Ian said, clapping his younger brother on the back.

WOLF HILLS INN proclaimed the wooden sign hanging from the porch roof of the two-story log building. Above the sign was a life-size carving of a wolf's head.

"Still much to be done, I fear. The tavern's already in use, but the rooms to let need a woman's hand."

"Byroney and I will see to that," Margaret Frazer said. "You did well, Duncan."

"Do we live here?" Nat asked, running up and down on the porch.

"The cabin to your left is where you'll be, lad," Duncan answered. "It was here when I bought the land, though I added some to it."

Byroney looked back at the wagons circled in the pasture at the foot of the hill. "This is a perfect place for weary travelers, Uncle Duncan."

Duncan snatched off his hat and bowed. "Glad you like it, Mistress Byroney. There's also a barn and pasture behind the inn, seven springs, and a bubbly bourn on the land."

"Creek," corrected By. "Bourns are called creeks in this country."

"And lochs are lakes," Duncan said, smiling. "New names for a new country, eh, By?"

"Let's not get into politics now," Mrs. Frazer said quickly. "Show us the house, Duncan."

Led by a chattering Nat, everyone trooped to the log cabin nestled among the trees a hundred yards from the inn.

Margaret Frazer was delighted with the spacious cabin, the huge, stone fireplace, and the divided sleeping loft. " 'Tis wonderful, Duncan. More than enough room for the seven o' us. Best of all, it is ours. A home of our own!"

"Thanks to your petticoats, you are landed gentry now," Duncan teased. "Laird and Lady Frazer, welcome to your estate."

"Duncan," Ian said sternly, "we have left all that behind us. There are no lairds and ladies on the frontier. Just common folk who wish to make a home for themselves."

"I was only funning, brother. A wee touch o' Scottish humor," Duncan said quickly. "What shall we do first, Maggie?"

Byroney was eager to explore the place, but her mother had other ideas. Margaret Frazer set everyone to work unloading the wagon, fetching, and carrying. By suppertime they were almost moved into their new quarters.

After gulping her cold supper, By said, "I'm off to say farewell to Charity and the others. They'll be gone come first light."

"Me, too," piped Nat.

"Don't let the Indians get you," warned Duncan.

Nat's eyes grew big as saucers. "Are there Indians, Uncle?"

"Duncan . . ."

"Sorry, Maggie. No, Nat. The Indians have been peaceable lately. I'll show you our new fort tomorrow when we go into town."

"I'm not afeared," Nat said, puffing out his chest. Nevertheless, he stuck to Byroney's side like molasses until they reached the circle of wagons.

Farewells were not easy, Byroney discovered. She'd made many friends on the long trek. They came from many places—Ireland, England, Wales, Scotland, and Germany. No two families alike. The one thing they all had in common was the dream of carving new lives for themselves and their families. "I hope their dreams come true," By said, trudging back to the cabin behind Nat.

"Who you talkin' to, By?" Colin asked from the cabin porch.

"Myself. Only way I can get a sensible answer. Where is everyone?"

"Ma's readin' for bed. Pa, Andrew, and Uncle Duncan are up to the tavern. I stepped out for a breath afore turnin' in. I'm plumb wore-out."

"It's been a tiresome, long day," By agreed. "I'm for bed. A real bed!"

The section of the sleeping loft partitioned off for her was small but cozy. She fell asleep almost as soon as her head hit the feather pillow.

Much later she was wakened by the sound of low voices. Creeping to the edge of the loft and peering down, she saw her father and her uncle having a heated conversation.

" 'Tis no use talking, Ian. I'll stay till you're settled, then I'm off."

"Why, mon? Look at the work you've put in. Now's the time to enjoy the fruits o' your labor. 'Tis your home, Duncan."

25

"It will be here when I return. Only better. For two years, I've itched to see what lies beyond the mountains. Poor as the trail through the Cumberland Gap is, settlers are pouring into Kaintuk. Lordy, Ian, there's already three good-sized settlements—Boonesborough, Harrodsburg, and St. Asaph."

"You want to see the wilderness before it disapears, eh?"

Duncan gave a short laugh. "No fear o' that, brother. There's far too much o' it. No, Ian, there's more than wanderlust pushin' me."

"What else then?"

"I'd no wish to alarm you and Maggie. Word's come that the Crown is rousing the northern tribes to prevent further settlement. The Shawnee attacked Boonesborough this month. We could be next."

Ian spat into the dying fire. "Fat George is protecting his backsides."

"Exactly. I've not joined the militia here, but I aim to fight for our independence."

"You think there'll be British troops on the frontier?"

"No. They're spread too thin already. They'll use the Indians for their dirty work. The Shawnee and Wyandotte were already angry at the Cherokee for giving away Kaintuk."

Ian Frazer sighed. "When do you leave, brother?"

"We have to keep the frontier open if we're to win this war. There's a party going from Long Island Settlement in Tennessee in four days. I'd like to join them."

"What do I tell the family?"

Duncan laughed. "Tell them I'm scratchin' my itchy feet. Or better yet, that I'm going on a Long Hunt come fall and will be back next spring with loads of furs and hides. No need to alarm them about the Indians."

26

"Aye. Me and the boys will join the militia soon as possible, too."

"A word o' caution, brother. There are English sympathizers about. Go wary, even o' other Scots. Some are ardent Tories."

"Not Highlanders! We never cottoned to the English heel!"

"Money speaks louder than blood to some. Be warned."

"Any names?"

"Only suspicions. The tavern will provide a good listening post."

As the men went off to bed, Byroney returned to her own. Sleep had vanished. Her head was filled with hidden Tories, marauding Indians, and fear for her beloved uncle. Admitedly, her fear was tinged with envy. Uncle Duncan was going into the Wilderness! And he'd get to fight for the Patriot cause. So would her pa and brothers. What could she do? Something ... She *must* do something. "I'll find a way," she murmured into her pillow. "This is Frazer land now. I'll not let anyone drive me from my home again."

No one said anything about last night's conversation the next morning. Uncle Duncan didn't mention his pending departure either. Byroney kept her own counsel as she pitched in beside her family getting matters in order.

"You're awful quiet," Colin said on a trip to the springhouse. "Reckon you miss Charity already. Or is it Buck?"

"Both. At least I got to say good-bye to Charity. Sam had Buck down at the blacksmith's."

"Don't fret. Sam'll be back through afore long. I heard Pa put a order in with him. Where Sam goes, Buck will go."

"Good." The news brightened her somewhat. She

liked the crusty Sam Cutter, and she was sure going to miss her daily rides.

" 'Spose I could have my clothes back now?''

"No! I might need them. You've outgrown them anyway. I bet you've grown two sizes of late, Colin Frazer.''

Colin threw out his chest, pleased. "Ma's not gonna let you run around here in breeches,'' he warned.

"I'll cross that creek when I get to it. I'm keeping the clothes, Colin.'' She marched into the house with a crock of cold milk.

General Washington had nothing on Margaret Frazer. She commanded her troops with skill and determination. For two days no one sat down, except to eat.

At supper on Saturday night, she looked over the exhausted band. "You've done good work. Tonight *everyone* will have a bath. Tomorrow we shall go to church and thank God for our good fortune.''

"I'll thank God for a day o' rest,'' Andrew whispered to By.

"Is there a church in Wolf Hills, luv?'' Ian teased. "I've been kept too busy to notice.''

"There's a church. We've been invited,'' Margaret replied. "Preacher stopped by yesterday. He's counting on all *seven* o' us.''

Ian looked at Duncan, who shook his head slightly. "Yes, luv. The Frazers will make their official appearance,'' he said meekly.

Sunday morning Ian Frazer hitched up the wagon— now minus its canvas top—and the Frazers rode to a log church in the center of the settlement.

Most of the hard wooden benches were filled by the time Preacher Tattersall rose to deliver his sermon. He was eloquent and very long-winded. Byroney's backsides were numb by the time they stood for the last hymn.

Once outside in the warm April sunshine, folk gathered around to greet the newcomers.

"Welcome to Wolf Hills. I'm Hiram Tipton. This is my family . . ."

"Welcome to Black's Fort. I'm . . ."

Andrew leaned down during a lull and whispered in By's ear, "Seems like they're o' two minds about what to call this place."

"Where'd all these folks come from?" By whispered back. "I didn't see that many houses." She shook more hands. Campbells, Shelbys, Craigs, Edmondsons, and Willoughbys flowed by in a bewildering tide.

"Byroney, I want you to meet someone special," her uncle said. "This is Will Atwood. His pa owns the Mercantile. Will's the one who carved our wolf head. He's got a special talent, has Will."

A pair of sky blue eyes peered shyly at By from under a shock of thick blond hair. "Welcome, Byroney."

"Thanks, Will. I love that wolf. Everyone comments on it. You're a true artist."

Before he could answer, Will was shouldered aside by a large man dressed in the height of Colonial fashion. "Don't encourage my son with his playtoys," he said, wagging a finger in By's face. "I have enough trouble keeping Will's mind on business without him thinking he's special."

Will flushed and seemed to shrink two sizes.

Byroney did not like fingers in her face any more than she liked to see people put down. "Why, Mr. Atwood, you surprise me," she said in her best Amelia-like voice. "Most men of culture would be proud to have an artist for a son."

Marcus Atwood's face turned bright red. "I'm p-proud

29

o' Will,'' he sputtered. He turned quickly and snapped his fingers. Immediately, two girls and a woman stepped forward. "These are my daughters, Miss Frazer, Mary and Margaret. Say howdy, girls."

The two well-dressed, pouty girls said in unison, "Welcome to Black's Fort." They didn't look as if they meant it.

"Isn't this nice, Mary–Margaret?" chirped a small, thin woman. "Another member for your sewing club! I'm Caroline Atwood, Byroney. Welcome."

Will shot her a grateful look as his father snapped his fingers again, and the Atwoods moved away.

"Mind your tongue, By," Andrew hissed. "The Atwoods are notables in Wolf Hills."

"Mr. Atwood's a tyrant," she hissed back.

The line of greeters kept coming. Luckily, Byroney met some other girls who she thought could be friends.

A ruggedly handsome man, about Andrew's age, was the last in line. Dressed in a plum frock coat, fawn knee breeches, and a snowy white shirt, he was like a peacock amongst doves. But it was his dazzling smile and twinkling dark eyes that caught and held By's attention. "Glad to have you in Wolf Hills, Miss Byroney," he said warmly when Andrew introduced him. "We've need of a little spice in our fair settlement."

"Thank you—I think—Mr. Kincaid," she replied, blushing under his teasing gaze.

"Evan, please. I understand from Sam Cutter you are quite a horsewoman."

Blast Sam Cutter! "Uh—yes, I do like to ride."

"Good. I'm always looking for an excuse to show off our community. Perhaps you'd allow me to accompany you?"

"I—I have no mount these days."

"I heard," he said, laughing. "Never fear, that can be remedied. Finding things for people is what I do best. Until later, Miss Byroney." He bowed over her hand and kissed it.

Speechless, Byroney watched him walk away. She noticed her eyes weren't the only ones following the progress of Evan Kincaid. Every woman—young or old—seemed to be aware of Mr. Handsome.

"Seems you have a gentleman admirer," Andrew teased.

Before she could respond, her father called, "Time to head home, Frazers. Duncan has something he wishes to tell us."

Duncan's announced departure threw everyone into a dither.

"You could enlist in the militia here like we're gonna do," Colin protested. "You don't have to run off to Kaintuk."

"Colonel Campbell says we've plenty to do right here," added Andrew.

"True enough. But three Frazers in Campbell's militia is more'n enough. Mostly, I want to explore. Now's the time. I'll be back next spring with a cache of furs and hides to add to the Frazer coffers," Duncan said. "Wish me luck, family."

They did. What else could they do? Duncan had given three years to make their dream come true. Fulfilling a personal dream was not amiss.

All six Frazers stood and waved until the tall, buckskin-clad figure rode out of sight.

"Duncan's always had wandering feet," Ian said. "Mayhaps this trip will get it out of his system and he'll settle doon."

Don't count on it, By thought. *Uncle Duncan's an adventurer.* Her own feet had a definite tingle in them.

Chapter 4

"**O**uch!" By dropped the hoe to inspect her latest blister. "You planted way too big, Mama," she complained, looking over the long rows of beans, onions, beets, potatoes, turnips, and corn.

"You'll be glad of every mouthful come winter," her mother replied. "Besides, we need extra to feed our guests."

Byroney sighed—audibly—and went back to chopping weeds. One of the first things her mama had done was plant a garden. Like everyone on the frontier, the Frazers had to grow their own comestibles and provender for their livestock. Yes, there was some bartering, but mostly you had to take care of yourselves. Garden duty fell to Nat, Ma, and her. "God must have a special fondness for weeds," she said, giving a vicious chop. "He sure made enough o' them. Maybe we could make Weed Stew for our guests."

Nat giggled. "We could season it with rocks. God must love rocks, too." He tossed another stone to the edge of the garden.

"Hurry along, you two," Mrs. Frazer called. "Best finish this afore this July sun bakes us brown as bread."

Looking at her golden arms and hands, By giggled.

32

"Lawsy me! What would Miss Amelia think o' my color?"

"Who cares?" Nat said. "She never had to feed herself or anybody else. Slaves did all the work at Burkeslea."

"I wouldn't trade places with her for all the tea in China," By retorted. "Reckon I'm not alone either. Look at how many folks are moving west."

It was true. The trickle of travelers along the Wilderness Road had turned into a flood that summer of 1777. The lower pasture was nearly always full of wagons. The inn rarely had an empty room. In fact, sometimes in bad weather, two or three people piled together in each space. Peter O'Doul, the man Uncle Duncan had hired to help run the place, said they could fill twice the number of rooms. Wolf Hills Inn was fast becoming an important rest stop for travelers.

At the end of the row, By stopped to stretch her back. "I'll sure be glad when Sunday comes."

"Why? You don't like our new preacher," Nat said. "Who said so?"

"You did. I heard you tell Belle Crabtree he was a long bag o' wind and short o' sense. Andrew thought that was right funny."

By made a futile grab for her little brother. "That was a private conversation, you big tattletale!"

Nat dodged and puffed his chest out like a bullfrog. "I'm not a tattler! You take it back."

"Are, too!"

"Children! Stop this foolishness. Byroney, go wash up and help Molly with the noon meal. Nat, if you've finished the beans, go do the corn."

Giving Nat a smirky smile, By took off. She loved taking her turn in the tavern. You met lots of different folks and heard all the news firsthand. She kept her ears open, too, remembering what her uncle had said about

Tories amongst them. So far, everyone seemed to support the Patriot cause. Besides that, the O'Douls, Peter and Molly, were fun. Everyone liked the lanky Irishman and his broad wife.

The hitching rail was full by the time she made her way to the tavern. "What's the fare today, Molly?"

"Slumgullion, for as long as it holds out. Bread, cheese, and pickles when that's gone."

For the next hour By and Molly were kept busy serving bowls of the fragrant stew and filling tankards of ale and cider.

The talk at every table was about the news a Mr. Randolph had brought earlier. The British General Burgoyne was leading an army of regulars, Hessians, and Indians down from Canada to take New York! General Washington was sending troops to engage him. It was widely felt that the British would be sent packing.

In the midst of this discussion, a scraggly man staggered in and headed for the bar. When Peter handed him a tankard, he threw back his head and drained it. " 'Nother!"

"That you, Jake Wilson?" someone called.

"Hit's me," the man replied, wiping his mouth on a greasy sleeve. " 'Nother."

"Mite early for that hard drinkin', ain't it?"

"Buryin's thirsty work. 'Specially the kind I done."

"Who'd you bury, Jake?"

"The Hodnuts. All seven o' 'em," Jake replied shakily. "Up t' Whisky Creek. Injuns got 'em. Scalped ever last one! Tortured 'em, too. Wust thing I ever seed."

The room fell silent as Jake Wilson described every gruesome detail.

"When this happen, Jake?"

"Four—five days ago, near as I could tell. I came on it day afore yesterday. Ain't slept since. Gotta get me to Fort Chiswell to tell the rest o' the Hodnut family. Damn them British!'' He staggered and held on to the bar.

Ian Frazer put a supporting arm around him. ''Easy, son. Thought you said Indians got them.''

''Boot tracks,'' Jake mumbled. ''Word *Whigs* splashed in blood. Injuns don't wear boots. Don't write neither . . .'' He passed out in Ian's arms.

''Help me get him upstairs,'' Ian said. ''Mayhaps he'll sleep now.''

''I'll see to his horse,'' volunteered Andrew.

Byroney hadn't moved since hearing the chilling tale. The words drew horrible pictures in her mind. Sometimes her vivid imagination was a curse.

Much to her surprise, the men silently drifted back to their tables and talk.

''What's the matter with you?'' she cried. ''Why aren't you going after those savages? Don't you care about seven slaughtered people?''

Every head in the room turned toward her.

''We care, Missy,'' one man said gruffly.

''Them Indians are long gone, Byroney,'' Peter said.

''That's the way o' them red devils. Hit-and-run.''

''What about the boot tracks? The writing? Why aren't you out looking for the Tory? How can you sit here like nothing's happened?'' She was beside herself with anger at these unfeeling men.

Collective anger and frustration flowed back at her.

Peter O'Doul put a hand on her arm. ''You'd understand had you been here longer, Byroney. We are not unfeeling, far from it. But 'tis foolish to set out on a old, cold trail. We've learnt that the hard way. There's too few o' us to waste our time fruitlessly.''

Peter's words made sense, but they didn't cool her outrage. Hands on hips, she glared at the men. ''Well, *something* should be done!''

''Aye, and something will, Battle Maid,'' her father

35

said, taking her elbow and guiding her gently toward the door. "You just leave matters to us men."

His words galled her. "This is my country, too. I have a right to speak out, same as any man."

Her father pushed her gently toward the steps. "Take a walk, Byroney. Cool down. Abe Johnson's gone to inform Colonel Campbell. The colonel will decide what action the militia will take. The Hodnuts will be avenged when we know the murderers."

Byroney shrugged away from her father's touch and marched off into the woods. How could those men sit there so calmly? Seven people had been horribly murdered. Not just by Indians either. The Tory message was loud and clear: Be a Whig and this could happen to you and your family. That threat made her so angry!

Stepping over the stones she'd placed in Deer Creek, By settled down in her secret place beneath the drooping branches of a huge willow. A place to be alone was hard to come by with a large family and a busy inn. She had discovered this place early on.

Gradually, the cool shade and gurgling water soothed her anger. She was still frustrated. She wanted to *do* something—be a part of the action. Women *should* play a part in this struggle for freedom. What could they do? Suddenly Sam Cutter came to mind! Why not do what Sam had done: teach the women to shoot. They could be trained to defend the fort, freeing up the men. That was it! A woman's brigade!

By jumped to her feet. "I'll ask the other girls at the church picnic on Sunday. They'll jump at the chance to be an active part of this war."

They laughed at her!

Mary and Margaret Atwood, the Shelby twins—Jessie and Jane, Agnes Craig, Emily Edmonson, Bessie Carriger, and Belle Crabtree had gathered around Byroney to hear the dramatic account of the brutal Hodnut slayings. But when she suggested they form a brigade to free up the men, they acted as if she were mad.

"Girls don't do things like that," scoffed Mary. "That's why we have menfolks."

"And Black's Fort," added Margaret.

"I can load for my pa," Agnes said, "but I'd never be able to fire a long rifle."

"Reckon I could, was I under attack," Belle said. "Probably couldn't hit the side of a barn, much less a Injun."

"You're just funnin' us, ain't you, Byroney?" Bessie said, grinning. "I know I'd look pretty silly astride a horse or tryin' to shoot. Injuns would laugh themselves to death a' seeing me try to do man's work." Bessie was a fairly large, rawboned girl.

Several girls giggled helplessly.

"I'm *not* being funny. Don't you want to be part of this war? Doesn't it rile you when the British use the Indians against us? What about this stinking Tory? You want menfolks always to do the protecting?"

The girls stepped back from Byroney's angry tirade and began drifting away.

All but one. Belle Crabtree put a hand on her arm. "Women do their share out here, By. When push comes to shove, I reckon we can do most anything. We don't let on to the menfolks 'bout it though. Ain't fashionable. It's kinda a game. We act weak and helpless and our men are brave protectors. They know they can count on us in trouble. Then, trouble over, we go back to weak and helpless. Understand?"

"I am *not* going to play that game."

Belle smiled. "You'll play. You're young and hotheaded, but you'll learn."

"And if I don't?"

"You'll be the prettiest old maid on the frontier. And you'll always be the best storyteller."

"Oh, Belle, be serious."

"I am. You had my hair standin' on end with that tale. You made it powerful real, By."

"Not real enough," By said with a sigh. "I'll have to come up with something better to shake those sillies awake."

Belle shook her head. "You're buckin' tradition. You won't win."

The bell for second preaching sounded, sparing By a reply. She and Belle rounded up the small children and took them to their parents. Byroney was still prickling from the rebuff.

Will Atwood came and sat beside her on the grass. "Been a nice day up to now."

By looked at the cloudless blue sky. "Still is."

"I see a thundercloud."

"Where?"

"On your face. You look mad as a wet hen, Byroney. Anything I can do?"

"You could talk some sense into your sisters! They're the leaders o' this bunch o' biddies."

Will laughed so loudly people turned to stare. "You ask a lot o' a fellow, don't you?"

Ignoring the glares, Byroney joined the laughter. "I guess that's like asking for the moon with those two."

"The moon might be easier," Will whispered, blushing as he noted the attention they were receiving.

"Ah-hem ... I will read from the Good Book: Psalms, twenty-three," boomed the preacher.

A hush fell over the assembled crowd as the beautiful, comforting words rolled out. The following sermon was short. After the last hymn, people began gathering their children and belongings for the trip home.

38

Will ignored his father's snapping fingers. "I wish you'd come to the Mercantile more often."

"Same distance both ways, isn't it?" By asked, smiling at his reddening face.

"Yeah, reckon so. You got a regular time off?"

"Most days I'm free from two to four."

"I'll see can Pa spare me long about then and come out."

"You do that." She watched with amusement as Will loped off after his father. He was a nice boy. Handsome, too. He had a great sense of humor and an even greater talent with his whittlin' knife. He'd sure be a lot more fun to talk to than those silly girls. Marriage, clothes, and gossip were all they ever wanted to discuss! They didn't seem to give a fig for whatever else was going on around them. Belle was the exception.

"Ma says shake a leg, By," Nat said, tugging on her skirt.

Byroney laughed. "I'd be willing to bet cash money that's not what she said, Nathaniel Frazer."

"Well, it was what she meant! 'Sides, I don't have no cash money."

"You don't have any money," By corrected.

"That's what I said!"

"Oh, it's impossible to tell you anything!"

Nat backpedaled just out of her reach. "Well, somebody told me *something*—about you. But I'm not a tattletale, like you said."

Feinting one way and going the other, By grabbed him. "What is it, Nat? Better tell."

Nat squirmed in her grasp. "Cain't! It's a surprise. Let me go, By."

"Byroney! Nathaniel! Hurry along," their mother called in a no-nonsense voice.

No amount of coaxing or threatening could get anything out of Nat, except, "I'm not a tattletale!"

It wasn't the first time Byroney's words had come back to haunt her. "Probably won't be the last," she said to herself. As punishment, all the way home she had to listen to Nat humming, "I-know-something-I-won't-tell."

By wanted to squeeze his scrawny neck!

Chaper 5

"Which do you like?"

By's heart thumped wildly as she looked at the two beautiful horses: one a lustrous black, the other a burnished red-gold. "They are both bonny, Evan."

"Choose. I can no afford both," her father said, smiling from ear to ear.

"Which one, Mama?"

Margaret Frazer shook her head. "Don't ask me. We have two good riding horses already. You're spoiling the lass, Ian."

"A promise is a promise, Maggie luv," Ian replied.

"I suspect the gelding—the black—has better bloodlines," Evan said. "The filly's a mixed, frontier breed. Both are well schooled."

Byroney was only half-listening. She rubbed their velvet noses. Brushing aside the filly's long, tan forelock, she gave an excited yelp. "Look, Papa! The filly's blaze looks like a Scottish thistle!"

"So it does," her father said, looking at the white mark between the filly's eyes.

"I'll take this one."

Evan looked puzzled, but handed her the halter rope. "Don't you want to ride them before you decide?"

By shook her head. "No, Evan. She has the mark o' Scotland on her. We'll do fine."

"I knew, and I didn't tell," Nat piped proudly. "What are you going to name her, By?"

"Liberty. From Mr. Henry's speech. Remember, Papa?"

"Ever the passionate Patriot," Evan said, joining in the laughter.

"Happy fifteenth birthday, Byroney," her father said. "Liberty's your responsibility. See you mind her well."

Byroney threw her arms as far as they would go around his great frame. "I will, Papa. Thank you, thank you. I'll never forget this day. Thank you, too, Evan, for finding Liberty. May I ride her now, Papa?"

"Go up to the barn. I expect Andrew can come up with a saddle."

"May I ride with you?" Evan asked.

"Yes! I'll go change." Ignoring her mother's look, By ran into the cabin. Quick as a wink, she dug out Colin's old clothes, dressed, grabbed her hat, and was back on the cabin porch. "Let's go, Evan."

To Evan's credit, he showed no surprise at her strange getup. "Ready and waiting, Miss Byroney."

"One caution," her father said sternly. "You're *never* to wander off into the mountains. Stay on the paths and roads. Do I have your solemn promise on that, Byroney Rose?"

"I promise, Papa."

A short time later as By and Evan were cantering down the Inn road they passed a figure trudging up the hill. By reined Liberty and trotted back. "Hi, Will. How do you like the horse Evan brought me? Her name's Liberty. Evan and I were just out for a trial ride."

"She's a beauty. Nice smooth gait, too. You're a perfect match."

42

"Were you coming to visit?" By asked, suddenly remembering her invitation.

"No. Just out for a walk and got thirsty."

"Want to come with us? You could saddle up Andrew or Colin's horse."

Will glanced over at Evan and shook his head. "Some other time, By. I better get on back to the store 'fore Pa throws a conniption."

"See you later, Atwood," Evan said. "Let's go, Byroney."

"Have a good ride," called Will.

Feeling a trifle guilty, By rode on. The guilt didn't last long. It felt too good being back in the saddle—on her own horse, too. Liberty was a nice little filly, with just enough spunk to make Byroney pay attention.

Evan was a good guide. He knew the names of roads and who lived along them. He had amusing gossip about each family, too.

"Do you know *everybody* hereabouts, Evan?"

"Have to in my trade."

"What exactly is your trade? I've heard one thing, then another."

"All good, I hope. I suppose you could call me a finder. I find out what folks want and get it for them. Sometimes I have to haul it from as far away as Pennsylvania or the Carolinas. Keeps me on the move."

"What if someone decides they don't want what you haul back?"

Evan laughed. "Well, it has happened, I grant you. But, like a cat, I always land on my feet. I've always been able to talk someone into buying the goods. There's always Marcus Atwood."

"Will's pa?"

"The same. Marcus thinks he's a shrewd businessman, but if you make anything sound pompous enough or scarce enough, he'll buy it."

43

Byroney giggled, then frowned. "He gives Will a hard time. About his carving, I mean."

"Will's no merchant, that's for sure. The boy's a dreamer, not a doer."

"We need dreamers as well as doers," By said sharply. "My brother Andrew dreams of nothing but running a huge flock of sheep on these hills."

"Aye, but Andrew has the guts to do something about his dream."

"What? What's Andrew doing?"

"My next trip out, I'm to look for a sheepdog for Andrew," Evan said with a laugh. "First the dog, Andrew says, then the sheep."

By had no idea Andrew was so quickly pursuing his dreams. Though all he ever talked about was those silly sheep, she hadn't paid him much mind. It irked her that a stranger knew more than she did. "And are you bringing Andrew his dog?"

"Aye. And the sheep, too, if he doesn't listen to reason."

"What reason?"

"Two actually. Wolves and bears. Andrew will not make his fortune with sheep. Not out here. Those pushing westward will find things different from what they expected, Byroney."

"Would you have us stay on the coast as King George ordered?"

"I did not say that, my passionate Patriot."

"That's twice you've called me that. Why?"

"What else would you call a fiery girl who wishes to form a woman's brigade?" Evan asked teasingly.

By felt her face glow. "Who told you?"

"I suspect Mary and Margaret were the first news-bearers. They're the source of most gossip."

"A pox on both of them! See if I ever include them again."

"Mind how you go, Byroney. Having those two for enemies would be a mistake."

"Oh pshaw! What can those two blabbermouths do to me?"

"Make you seem a fool. Reputation is everything. They're already jealous of you."

"Jealous? Of what?"

Evan threw back his head and laughed so hard his horse danced sideways. "You really don't know?"

By shook her head, bewildered.

"Those two are envious of your beauty and your ease with people. You've challenged their status as queens of these hills."

"I've done no such thing!" She wasn't used to compliments. Evan flustered her. To cover her confusion, she kicked Liberty into a gallop and rode for home.

She had unsaddled and was cooling Liberty by the time Evan rode up to the barn.

"Thank you for the ride, Miss Byroney," Evan said formally. "I'm off to the Carolinas on the morrow. Anything I can fetch for you? Perhaps another riding outfit?"

"You've brought me quite enough, thank you," By replied, refusing to meet his eyes. "Have a good journey."

"Don't forget to search for my order," Andrew said, stepping from the barn shadows.

"I'll find you a good dog, Andrew. Good day, Frazers."

Byroney watched him ride away. She rather hoped he'd be gone for a long spell. Something about Evan Kincaid rattled her.

"Don't stand there woolgathering, By. Ma's looking for you."

"Would you put Liberty up, Andrew? I better go." Quickly, she made her way to the cabin.

"Did you forget the time?" Ma asked sharply. "Having your own horse doesn't mean you can neglect your chores."

"Yes, Mama."

"Will Atwood left a package for you. I put it on the steps."

By ran inside and carefully opened the clumsily wrapped package. Suspended on a thin blue ribbon was a delicate quarter moon carved from a highly polished piece of wood.

"What is it?" Mrs. Frazer asked as By burst out laughing.

"The moon," By answered, holding the necklace up. "Will gave me the moon."

"What's so funny? It's a lovely piece."

"It's a private joke twixt Will and me. It is bonny. I'll thank Will next time he comes around."

"See that you do. Now, run change into some decent clothes."

Chuckling at Will's cleverness, By hastened to obey.

When a week passed and Will had not come to the Inn, By decided to take matters into her own hands. "I'm riding into town, Mama. Need anything?"

"I'm almost out of brown thread. You could pick up a spool for me."

"All right. I wanted to thank Will anyway."

Several people were in the store and only Marcus Atwood behind the counter. Byroney waited for a lull, then asked, "Is Will about, Mr. Atwood?"

"No. He's off tramping through the woods somewheres, looking for pieces o' wood," he answered, mockingly.

"Thanks." By left before she said something smart. She made her way through the crowded aisles, almost

46

to the door, before she remembered the brown thread. Sighing, she retraced her steps.

"Who was that lad?" asked a male voice. "Don't recollect seeing him about."

"Lad?" Mr. Atwood said with a cruel laugh. "That was no lad! 'Twas the innkeeper's daughter."

"Disgraceful! Immodest!" a woman chimed in. "A young woman showing off her limbs in such a fashion! What must her mother be thinking?"

"That one has a mind o' her own," Mr. Atwood replied. "Did you hear her silly notion of a woman's brigade?"

"Lordy, what's that?"

"Just a way to call attention to herself," the woman replied with a haughty sniff.

Face burning painfully, Byroney backed out of the store. She didn't trust herself to speak . . . if she could have found the words. She hadn't meant to show off anything! Never thought she had anything to show. Breeches were just more comfortable than skirts. It was clear that Mary and Margaret weren't the only gossips in Wolf Hills. She swung into the saddle and galloped off. Away from town, tavern, and everyone!

She'd only gone a little way when she spied the Atwood buggy coming toward her with Mary and Margaret aboard. Hastily, she turned Liberty onto a side road and galloped on. She had no desire to see anyone at the moment, especially not those two. Then, a short distance away, she heard a wagon rumbling along!

"Drat! Is there no place to be alone?" She swung her horse off the lane and into the woods.

Liberty seemed more than happy to go at a slower pace in the cool of the forest. For more than an hour they rambled up one faint track and down another. For a time, Byroney was lost in her misery, but gradually she became aware of the beauty around her and began to enjoy her surroundings. A rich, piney aroma perfumed the air. Birds chirruped, small animals scurried and chattered as they ambled past. It was cool and peaceful in these deep, dry woods. Coming upon a stream, she dismounted, drank, and gave Liberty a watering. "Reckon I'm over my mad, girl. Guess we better head on home," she said, remounting.

Twenty minutes later she came to the stream again. The same spot! Her tracks and Liberty's were plain to see in the soft mud. A small chill rippled down her spine. "Guess we kinda went in a circle, girl. Let's try again."

The chill became a numbing, heart-pounding freeze when Byroney realized she was hopelessly lost. Nothing seemed familiar. One tree looked much like another. There were no tracks to follow on the pine floor of the forest. Panic seized her. The woods closed in around her like a giant fist. She wanted to kick Liberty into a gallop and go . . . go anywhere but here. The urge to flee was almost overwhelming. . . .

They broke through the woods into a clearing. Towering above them was a tall, craggy outcrop of rocks, pointing skyward like giant fingers. "Bet I could get a good view from up there, Liberty. See Wolf Hills, maybe. Leastwise, I'd have a better idea of where in thunder we are." She dismounted and tied her horse in the shelter of trees.

On shaky legs, she began climbing the rocky slope. It was steeper than she thought. Once on top, she gasped, "Oh, Lordy!" Miles and miles of mountains rolled before her in a continuous green wave. There was no sign of Wolf Hills . . . or any other habitation. "M-Maybe from t-the other s-side . . ."

Coming around a boulder, she had another surprise. The finger rocks curled around a small, lush green area. "A fairy bowl!" For a moment her fear was replaced with delight. In Scotland finding such a spot was the best of good luck. And if you caught the fairies dancing, they had to grant you a wish! "I'm too old to believe in fairies." Nevertheless, she stood stock-still, waiting.

In the silence she heard the pounding of footsteps . . . many footsteps. A warning bell went off in her head. She dived for cover under a tangle of rhododendron as the slap-slap-scritch-scritch came closer . . . closer . . .

Chapter 6

I ndians!

Hardly daring to breathe, Byroney watched as a flood of bronze men with fierce, painted faces filled the fairy bowl. Silently, they hunkered down, waiting.

At a barked command, one warrior spread himself on a flat rock, watching the trail they'd just come up. The silence of such a large group was eerie.

After what seemed an eternity, the fiercest-looking Indian rose and came straight toward her hiding place. It wasn't his looks that made the gorge rise in Byroney's throat. It was what he had dangling from his waist: two, tangled, bloody mats of hair! One had blond pigtails ... By swallowed the bitter liquid, taking in small sips of air. She could *not* vomit now!

Inches from her nose, the moccasined feet halted. By closed her eyes and waited for death.

Instead, there was a soft exchange of words and the feet moved away.

By opened her eyes in time to see the lookout on the rock slither down. Then, as silently as they had come, the Indians departed.

Several minutes passed before By could make herself move. When she scrambled out of the bushes her legs refused to support her and she sat back down with a thud. Taking deep gulps of air, she scanned the forest below her. Nothing! Had she dreamed this fearful nightmare?

Below her sunlight flashed on metal. Squinting, By saw another flash. The war party seemed to be moving in the direction where she thought Wolf Hills lay! She had to raise the alarm!

Keeping low, she half scooted, half crawled down the mountain.

Liberty was waiting, peacefully munching on the nearby grass.

Byroney jumped into the saddle. "We have to warn folks, Liberty. Take me home!"

Rested, Liberty responded to her urgency, and they took off at an angle to the Indians' path. Speed was not possible through the dense growth, yet she urged her horse faster and faster. Was that a trail? Go left? Right? Straight? Images of burned homesteads and scalped people spurred her onward. Branches of trees grabbed at her. Briars snagged her. Still, she kept going.

Finally, they burst from the woods. In the distance Byroney saw a tiny sliver of a road and recognized where she was. Twenty minutes later, a bedraggled figure on a lathered horse rode up to the Inn screaming, "INDIANS!"

People spilled from the tavern as By slid from her mount. "War party . . . headed this way!"

"How many? Which direction?" asked Captain Eggleston of the militia.

"A whole passel! South, I think. They had *scalps*!"

Captain Eggleston dispersed men in a well-rehearsed routine before turning to Byroney again. "Where did you spot the Indians?"

Byroney swallowed hard, looking at her pa. "In the mountains south o' Wolf Hills."

"Can you be more specific? Describe the mountain? How far out? How long ago? Mounted or on foot?"

"The mountain had a rocky peak, like giant fingers. I don't know how far . . . I was lost and tryin' to get home." She glanced up at the sky. "Maybe two hours? They were on foot, but moving fast."

"I'll see to you later," Pa said, mounting the horse Colin brought around. "Andrew, you and Peter prepare the Inn. Bring in any travelers." He and Colin rode off with Eggleston and the militia.

Mrs. Frazer put an arm around By's shaking shoulders. "Come along and get cleaned up. You're a mass of scratches. You ride through a briar patch?"

"I—I don't remember." By let herself be led to their cabin.

The whole settlement remained on high alert for two days. No trace of any Indians was ever found.

Ian Frazer was furious with his daughter. "You broke your word, Byroney Rose. I'm half-a-mind to sell that horse o' yours."

"I'm sorry, Papa. I was angry and didn't think. I didn't mean to disobey. Please, don't sell Liberty."

"You'll no ride her for a month! Is that understood?"

"Yes, Papa," By said, meekly and gratefully.

She did not get off so easily with Captain Eggleston, who refused to let the militia stand down until he was certain the danger was past. He came out to question Byroney once again. "Tell me exactly where you saw these fierce warriors, Miss Byroney."

"I told you all I can remember. They completely filled the fairy bowl!"

"Pardon?"

By blushed and tried to explain. The look on the captain's face and on those gathered around made her cringe. "I saw them, I tell you!"

"Maybe they was fairies," one man said, chuckling.

"Or ghost Indians," added another man. "I hear tell they's a lot o' 'em hereabouts."

"Yup, almost enough to fill a fairy bowl."

Byroney fled to the cookhouse—followed by laughter. It was bad enough having her father angry, but now folks thought she was seeing things! Or making them up.

As soon as the noon crowd thinned, she took off for her willow tree to nurse her wounds.

Will Atwood intercepted her. "Howdy, By. Where you off to?"

"Anywhere I can get shut o' this teasing," she snapped, trying to edge past.

"Mind if I tag along?"

By sighed. No use turning away a friendly face. "Come if you like. That is, if you aren't afraid to be seen with me. I wanted to thank you for my beautiful necklace, Will. I treasure it."

Will's face turned cherry red. "It weren't nothing. And I'm never afraid to be seen with you, Byroney."

By's bad mood was vanishing rapidly under Will's sincere gaze. "Might ruin your reputation t' be seen with a gal who sees things that aren't there."

"If you say you saw Indians, then you saw Indians," Will answered stoutly.

"Then why didn't the militia find them? Not one single trace of any Indians!"

"You reckon them Indians didn't want to be found? There's a heap o' land out there," Will said, waving an arm at the mountains.

In spite of herself, By shivered. She'd had nightmares about those trackless, green hills. "I know. A body could get lost forever in them."

"Some do," Will said, falling into step with her.

"Not me. Not ever again. I'm not going out there even when I get Liberty back."

"Did you lose Evan's present?" Will asked.

"Evan's present? Evan didn't give me Liberty! Pa bought her for my birthday. Whatever gave you that idea?"

"You did. I thought when we met on the road you said Evan *bought* her for you," Will said, grinning from ear to ear. "I thought that meant you was a courtin' couple."

"I'm not courting anybody, you silly gander," By replied. "Reckon I was so excited I just ran my words together. Come on, Will, let's walk by the creek. Walking's all I'll be doing for the next month."

Will grinned. "That's not so bad, By. A person sees a lot more walking than riding anyways."

"Like what?"

"Come with me, and I'll show you a chinquapin grove, a mayapple patch, and a real bee tree." Without further ado, he led her off into the woods beside the Inn to explore.

Will came out several times a week during the next month. Twice he snuck his pa's carriage and fetched Belle out for a visit.

"You're a good friend, Will," By said on the last day of her punishment.

"Glad I'm good for something," Will replied glumly.

"What's the matter?" By asked, noting his hangdog face for the first time.

"I messed up another order. Pa blistered my ears. Can't say as how I blame him. I ordered fourteen bolts o' blue calico instead o' four. Lordy, I don't reckon I'll ever be much o' a merchant."

"Probably because you hate it. If you had your druthers, what would you like to do, Will?"

"I'd like to make things out o' wood. Tables, chairs, beds, mirrors, chests. Beautiful things for folks to use and enjoy."

"Then do it."

Will shook his head. "I can't."

"Why not?"

"Lots o' reasons. For one thing, Pa's got his heart set on our sign reading: Atwood & Son. Since I'm the only son, that's me. Secondly, I don't know enough about fine woodworking. I'd need to apprentice myself to a cabinetmaker, like the man I met in Charleston. It would take me years. Pa would never let me go. He says cabinetmakers are common folk, not professionals like merchants."

Looking at Will's sad face made her angry. "How old are you, Will Atwood?"

"Seventeen, come spring. Time to put away my toys, Pa says, and become a man."

"You already are a man, Will. A good one. You can decide for yourself what you want to do."

Will shook his head. "No, I can't. Can't let Pa down. Having a fine, big store with his son has always been Pa's dream."

"What about your dream?"

Suddenly, Will smiled. "Ah, pay me no mind, By. I'm still smartin' from the tongue-lashing. I'll buckle down and become a good merchant. You'll see."

No amount of cajoling would change Will's mind. He was going to be a merchant like his Pa wanted whether or not he liked it. By finally gave up on sweet Will's ever having any backbone.

October dressed the mountains in a thousand hues of red and gold. Byroney was delighted with her first mountain autumn.

"Best enjoy it whilst you can," Molly warned. "The critters are awful busy gathering. This morning I saw a woolly worm with three large stripes!"

"So?"

"So we're in for a hard winter. Least three big snows afore spring."

"Oh pshaw! Who believes those old wives' tales?"

"I do. I've lived long enough to know. I got Peter bringing in extra firewood."

"Today? Nothing bad can happen on a beautiful day like today!"

Molly crossed herself and looked about fearfully. "Don't tweak the Devil's nose, Byroney. You'll hear bad news afore nightfall."

By hugged the rotund Molly. "Never fear, Molly. I'll have no truck with Old Scratch."

That evening Molly's prediction came true.

Byroney was serving Colonel Campbell and the other militia leaders when a red-faced youth came stumbling up to their table. He saluted smartly. "Colonel Campbell, Jeffry Daniels reporting from Fort Chiswell. Colonel Trears's compliments, sir." He handed over a folded dispatch.

The inn grew silent while Colonel Campbell read.

"What news, sir?" a man asked, looking fearfully at the colonel's grim face.

"Gentlemen, I'm sorry to report General Washington engaged General Howe at Brandywine Creek in Pennsylvania and was defeated. Philadelphia has fallen. Congress has fled to York, Pennsylvania."

Loud groans issued from every throat.

"Never fear. General Washington will fight back," young Daniels said stoutly.

There were hearty mutters of agreement and Colonel Campbell ordered cider all around.

"I fear this news will embolden the Tories in our midst," Colonel Campbell was saying when Byroney returned with a loaded tray.

"We'll watch our backs," the visiting Colonel Sevier promised.

Byroney made a promise, too. She would not tweak the Devil's nose ever again.

All the news coming into Wolf Hills wasn't bad that bright and beautiful autumn. Sam Cutter stopped by with word that Duncan Frazer was alive and prospering in Kaintuk.

"You saw him, did you?" Ian asked anxiously.

"I did. He's fared well, Ian. Duncan's jined up wi' Jericho Jones, the best hunter, trapper, and scout in these mountains. He'll come back a wiser, richer man."

"Now, Sam, I thought you were the best at all those things," By teased.

"Naw, reckon I be only third best if the truth's told," Sam said, looking sorrowful. "Boone's first, then Jones, then me."

"Only third out of all the men on the frontier? Why it's a wonder you got us here at all," By said. "As a reward for your efforts I'll show you my pride and joy. If you'll come on to the barn with me."

Sam's eyebrows shot up. "Lord-a-mercy, Miss Byroney! You keep your husband in th' barn?"

"My horse, you ninny!" By shouted over her family's laughter.

"Now don't get riled," Sam said. "I was only funnin' you. I won't even tell Buck you got a new love."

"You'll stay for supper?" Mrs. Frazer asked.

"I'd be obliged. Lead on, Missy." But in spite of the Frazer's pleadings, Sam wouldn't stay longer. "Gotta git over t' my place and git me ready fer winter. Hit's gonner be a big 'un," he warned. "Y'all best git ready fer it."

This time Byroney held her tongue.

⌒⌒⌒

Chapter 7

In spite of word of Washington's defeat at German-town, late October found the settlement in a festive mood. Autumn was the social season. People came together for work and play. There were work gatherings such as corn huskings, apple butter runs, hog slaughters with sausage makings, and quilting bees. By liked the social parties best: the Bespoke Parties for newly engaged couples, square dances, and community sings.

Byroney was enjoying every moment of the square dance at Haley's barn. "Whew! I'm plumb tuckered," she said, flopping on a hay bale beside Belle after a vigorous reel.

"You should be. You danced purt-near every set. Look-a-here! Both Will and Evan are a bringin' you cider."

Evan reached Byroney first. "You look as if you could use this."

"Thank you. I'm bone dry."

Will handed Belle his extra cider. "Your Pa plays a mean fiddle, Byroney."

"Wait till you hear his bagpipes!"

Will shook his head. "Druther not."

"Why?" Evan asked, raising one dark eyebrow. "Don't you like the pipes?"

"Oh, I like 'em well enough," Will replied. "It's just they signal the end o' the party. I haven't had enough dancing with Byroney. Can I have this one?"

"Certainly."

Will whirled her into a set. Evan and Belle joined them.

"You going to the Masons' corn husking?" Belle asked when she and By begged out of the next set and Will and Evan were snatched away.

"Ma mentioned it. What are you taking to Josie and Jane's Bespoke party?"

Belle leaned close and whispered, "If I could wrap up luck, I'd take a big box o' it."

By giggled. "The Snyder boys aren't much of a catch, are they?"

"The Snyders got right much land. Each boy gets a passel to hisself. Makes them more attractive than they look."

Byroney watched the two scraggly Snyder men twirling the petite Shelby twins around the floor. "Floyd's a lot older than Josie, isn't he?"

Belle nodded. "Floyd's been married afore. First wife died in childbirth. Ma said Floyd run off huntin' knowing Estelle was due any minute. Ma sent Floyd packing when he come sniffin' around me two years ago."

"Two years ago? You'd have been just a child, Belle!"

"I was old enough for Floyd's purpose," Belle said, laughing. "Life's hard on women out here. Girls marry young and die young. You'll see."

"Well, I don't aim to do either!"

"Do what?" Evan asked, coming up beside her.

Byroney tossed her auburn curls. "'Marry or die."

Evan threw back his head, laughing. "My sentiments

exactly, Miss Byroney. We're a perfect pair. May I have this dance?" Without waiting for an answer, he swept her away.

By glanced over her shoulder and saw shy Tom Jenkins finally making his way toward Belle, but before he arrived someone else whisked her away. Unmarried females were in short supply.

"I wish it could be autumn all year," By said, as their wagon rattled homeward. "Except for Sunday meeting, it's the only time you get to see folks."

"You took to dancing like a duck to water," her father said proudly. "All the Frazer clan have music in them."

"Hah! You can no take all the credit, Ian Frazer," Margaret Frazer said. "The McLeods are widely known for their pipers and dancers."

"And why do you think I wed you? Sure and it wasn't just your lovely face!" Ian put an arm around his wife and drew her closer.

Byroney watched her parents snuggle. If *and* when *I ever marry,* she thought, *that's the kind of love I want. Both of them are strong-willed, independent people, yet they pull together just like our draft horses, Bonnie and Donald.*

Not everyone was pulling together it seemed. One night Colonel Campbell announced a major blow to the Patriot militia. "Word's come the Johnsons and Skaggs over in Cedar Valley were burned out by Tories last week. No lives were lost, but we did lose the store of ammunition and supplies hidden at their places."

"A magazine at Alf Johnson's?" Evan asked. "Fancy that! I believe I stayed at the Johnson place on my last trip to Carolina."

"Everyone stays there, Kincaid," Marcus Atwood said. "I've done so myself."

"We had the supplies well hid. Somebody betrayed us," Colonel Campbell said. "They knew where our cache was hidden and took it before they burned the place to the ground."

"You certain it was Tories?" someone asked. "I hear the Cherokee are short o' shot for their rifles. Purdy riled about it, too. Little Carpenter's havin' a hard time holdin' 'em in line."

Byroney had lingered as long as she dared around the table. With the last of the tankards gathered, she set off for refills and missed the last of the discussion. The idea of a traitor amongst them had her riled for fair.

As By and her pa closed the tavern that evening, she said, "Pa, why would anyone be a Tory? Why set against your neighbors? And freedom to govern yourself? I just don't understand!"

"Power and wealth speak with loud voices, lass. Some are betting against us winning this war. They've thrown their lot in with the rich and powerful British. They pretend to support our cause and betray us at every turn."

"Someone who loves power and wealth, eh? Like Marcus Atwood?"

"Guard your tongue, lass! Misliking a man is no cause for such accusations. Neither is ambition. If that were so, half o' us would stand accused."

"Sorry, Pa. What are we doing about these ... Tory snakes?"

"The best we can. 'Tis not easy. They're a clever bunch."

Thinking of the serpents in her garden, By had trouble getting to sleep. She ran through every man she knew and could think of nothing suspicious. It had to be a man! No woman would betray friends and family. Besides, women didn't move about unnoticed. ... Ah, there was a thought! Perhaps women could flush out this traitor quicker than men. By pounded her pillow into a more comfortable position. "I'll talk this idea over with Belle tomorrow."

The next afternoon she rode Liberty to the Crabtree place. As soon as she had Belle alone, she poured out the story of betrayal and her plan.

"You're a caution, Byroney Frazer. I reckon this would work summat better than your woman's brigade. But most women are stuck on their place, except for Sundays. How are they gonna find a traitor?"

"People come by, don't they? Women are more observant. We note little things. At least, say you'll keep your eyes peeled, Belle."

"I'll do that all right. That kind o' varmit should be hanged."

"I'd make the weddy myself!"

"Weddy? What on earth's that?"

"A noose, you goose!" By replied, laughing at Belle's puzzled look. "A hangman's noose."

"Well, there'll be others in line afore you. We don't cotton to turncoats."

"I know," By said with a sigh. "I just want to help our cause. I'm gonna ask the other girls to keep an eye out."

"Uh . . . By, I wouldn't do that, was I you. Let's keep this twixt us."

"Why? Don't it make your blood boil to think of someone you know betraying you?"

"Sure as shootin'! But you don't want your name spread all over Wolf Hills, like before, do you? Folks already think you're . . . well, a mite het up on things."

"I sure wouldn't want our plan spread all over Wolf Hills," By said thoughtfully. "I reckon you're right."

"I know I am. You're in the best spot anyways. You see a heap more folks than most."

Disappointed, By glanced up at the sky. "Guess I better mosey back. Those clouds look threatening."

"It's gonna weather," Belle agreed. "Ma's rheumatiz is acting up something fierce."

"I had an even better sign this morning," By said, laughing. "Tam, Andrew's sheepdog, rounded up Ma's chickens!"

Belle laughed. "Bet your critters will be glad when Tam gets sheep to herd."

"Like as not, Tam'll still herd everything in sight. See you at the Atwoods' Sewing Circle?"

"If the weather holds."

The weather did not hold. A blast of icy air turned the rain to sleet and then to snow. The first blizzard of the season locked eyeryone in a prison of white.

As Washington's army went into winter quarters at Valley Forge, the Frazers hunkered down in Wolf Hills until the long, cruel winter of '77–'78 passed.

True to her word, By kept her eyes and ears open for likely traitors. No one betrayed himself by word or deed. It was very frustrating. There seemed to be no way at all she could contribute to the fight for freedom. These Tories were indeed slippery creatures!

Chapter 8

In the second week of spring thaw, Byroney was picking her way across the mud-logs between the cabin and the inn when she spied a scraggly, bearded man coming up the road, leading three pack mules. "Uncle Duncan!"

Ignoring the muck, she hiked up her skirts and ran to greet him.

Duncan enfolded her in a bear hug. "You need a boulder on your head, lass. You've all growed up."

Byroney stood back, wrinkling her nose. "And you need a wash!"

A grin flashed beneath the thick, red beard. "I see no one's thrown a bridle on your tongue yet. What news since I left?"

"Ma and Pa are well. The Inn's doing tolerable—though summat slow this awful winter. Andrew's making calf eyes at Demity Logan. She's the only thing he thinks about, except sheep. Colin hasn't changed overmuch. Nat's another story. He's growing so fast Ma can't keep him in britches . . ."

"And you?"

"I worked in the tavern room this winter. Molly's sciatica's acting up. Peter's teaching me to play the Irish harp. I love it! Oh, Pa bought me a horse! Liberty's the prettiest thing you ever did see. Ma even made me a riding skirt, so's I don't shock folks. What about you?''

"I have tales to tell, never fear. But they must wait till I've said my howdys, washed, and slept for a week.''

Before By could protest, Ian came out looking for her. "Duncan!" he roared. "I'd almost given up on you.''

The Inn and cabin emptied at Ian's bellow. Happy confusion reigned.

Finally, Duncan untangled himself. He handed the mules' lead ropes to Nat. "Will you see to these fellows, Nat? Go careful with the load. 'Tis worth a fortune.''

"I'll help him, Uncle Duncan," volunteered Colin. "Have you sold up yet?''

"No. Do you know a trader going out?''

"Got a fellow leaving tomorrow. Evan Kincaid will get you a fair price. Reckon he'd take your wares," Ian answered.

Staggering slightly, Duncan said, "Would you see to it, brother? I'm fair wore-out.''

"Aye, that I will.''

Margaret Frazer plucked Duncan's sleeve. "Come along now. By the time you're clean, food and bed will be waiting.''

With a wee lad smile, Duncan let himself be led away. And By had to wait for her report on the wilderness.

When Duncan emerged two days later he did indeed have stories to tell. "Kaintuk is a grand and glorious land . . . once you get there. Boone's road through the Gap is hardly more than a footpath! But you dasn't get off it—not lest you know how to push through canebreaks, ford streams, tramp up and down trackless, thick forest without losing your way. I finally learnt t'do such, but not afore I chased myself in circles a few times.''

Byroney shivered, remembering her journey in the mountains. "What about when you got through?"

"It can rightly be called the Promised Land: rolling hills; lush, fertile soil; good water; stands of walnut, cherry, and sugar maples. Settlements have sprung up like mushrooms. 'Course, the Indians don't cotton to that! Settlers are under constant threat of attack.''

"Nothing worth having comes easy," Ian said. "How'd you come by those furs? Kincaid says they're the best he's seen.''

"The land's full o' game: buffalo, bear, beaver, deer, and fox. Jericho and me never wanted for meat. Meal and greens run short though,'' Duncan replied, helping himself to more biscuits. "Reckon Kincaid'll fetch us a good price?"

"Evan's the best fur trader hereabouts,'' By blurted. Then seeing the looks on her brothers' faces, added, "Or so some say.''

"Evan's courtin' By," piped Nat.

"He is *not*! We go riding together, that's all.''

Colin grinned. "And dancing, and singing,'' he added.

"Don't leave out Will Atwood,'' Andrew said. "Will's dancing on By's string, too.''

"Least I don't go mooning like a orphan calf, as some I could name,'' By shot back.

"Whoa, now. I see I got lots o' catching up to do,'' Duncan said quickly. "No time now though. Better us get to work.''

"You're right, brother. Morning's half gone,'' Ian said.

Giving Andrew a baleful glare, By stomped out to do her chores. What was wrong with everybody? Was courting and marriage all anyone could think about?

What was wrong with friendship? She liked watching Will carve his wooden animals. Wood came alive in his hands. He was fun and a good listener. Evan, on the other hand, was fun to listen *to*! Evan had gone places, met people, and done things. He had schemes and dreams. 'Course it didn't hurt having the two best-looking men in Wolf Hills for friends. She loved the green looks Margaret Atwood threw her way. Now there was one eager to wed!

"Well, I'm not," By said to her broom. "And I'm not about to change."

Many things did change that summer of 1778. For one thing, it rained . . . and rained . . . and rained. The ground, already soaked by winter snows, could not absorb more moisture. Streams and rivers overflowed. Gardens did not flourish. Travelers and wagons were stuck in the miry muck that passed for a road. Yet still they came. Wolf Hills Inn was never in want of guests. The Frazers were busier than ever.

Byroney had no time to think, much less alter any of her feelings.

Seeing the constant flood of settlers taking their lands and hunting grounds, renegade bands of Cherokee struck the outlying cabins with a vengeance. On one such raid, they captured Eliza Adams and her three children.

Byroney's father and brothers were in the militia that set out to bring the captives back. They caught up with the Indians at Rattlesnake Creek. The Adams family was rescued, but Colin took an arrow in his left arm. It was only a flesh wound, but it brought fear into Byroney's heart.

A hero's welcome awaited the militia on their return to Abingdon—as Wolf Hills was now officially called.

"You do not look happy, Byroney," Evan said, handing her a cup of cider at the celebration.

"Colin gave me a scare. Besides, with all the men away, Duncan, Mama, and I have worked nonstop. I'm too tired to celebrate. Even my hair aches with weariness, Evan."

"I have some news that will cheer your Patriot heart. Washington's holding Clinton in New York! The war goes well for us in the north."

"That is good news! Have you told Colonel Campbell?"

"I just rode in last night. I expect he already knows though. Surprising as it is, word travels fast on the frontier."

"Go make certain," By ordered. "This is truly cause to celebrate."

Evan saluted smartly. "Yes, General."

"Sent him packing, did you?" inquired a familiar voice. "That mean you've made a choice?"

By whirled and embraced Belle. "I've been looking all over for you! You haven't been to meeting in weeks."

"Ma caught the consumption this spring. She's still poorly. You ain't been by neither," Belle said, hugging By hard.

"Pa and the boys were off. I had double duty. What choice?"

Before Belle could answer, a fiddle began and Tom Jenkins and Will came up and swept them into a set.

Byroney didn't see Belle again until the celebration was over and folks were heading home.

"Come over soon," Belle invited as the Crabtree wagon pulled out.

"I'll try, but Andrew and Pa are going up the Shenandoah Valley for sheep."

"Come when you can. I get lonesome for company," Belle begged.

And I could do with a little less, By thought. Aloud, she said, "I'll come. I promise."

Sometimes promises are hard to keep. It was a full three weeks before Byroney found time to slip away for a quick visit.

The Crabtree homestead had a ragged, forelorn look that July afternoon. "Belle! Belle, are you t'home?" By called.

"Out back."

By tied Liberty to the porch rail and went around to the back of the house. Zelda Crabtree sat propped in an old rocking chair, a pan of shelly beans in her lap. Around her sat Belle and six other little Crabtrees, all with pans of sorry-looking beans.

"Howdy, By," Miz Crabtree said in a whisper. "Belle said you was a comin' by. Come set a spell."

By was shocked by the woman's wasted appearance. Nevertheless, she smiled and sat. "Pass me a batch. I'll shell whilst I visit."

"Fetch us a cold bucket o' water, Lonnie," Belle requested. "Sorry we caint offer you nothin' else. The cow went dry."

"Nothing's better than water on a hot day," By replied. "Milk clogs a body's throat."

Whether it was because of the extra hands or her prattle of news and gossip, Byroney wasn't sure, but the pile of beans diminished rapidly.

"Y'all run on have a visit," Miz Crabtree said, nodding at Belle and By. "I'm gonna lay me down fer a spell. You younguns be quiet now, y'hear."

"Let's go sit round front in the shade and jaw," Belle invited.

"How long's your ma been like this?" By asked as soon as they were settled.

"Since March. Cold went to her chest. She's been coughin' blood."

"Lord-a-mercy! Why didn't you let me—or somebody—know? We could have helped out," By said.

Mountain pride bristled in Belle's reply. "We're makin' do. Don't need charity."

"Helping neighbors isn't charity! You know that, Belle Crabtree."

Belle's shoulders sagged. "That's what I told Pa. He don't see it thataway. We got no way to repay a kindness. You best not blab, Byroney. Get me in a heap o' trouble."

Byroney had come to know, and admire, the proud, independent spirit of her frontier neighbors. They'd give you the shirt off their backs in a snowstorm, but wouldn't accept a handout from anyone. This situation was ridiculous though. "At least let me send out the new doctor in town. He's German, and you can't hardly understand him, but he's helped other folks."

"Dr. Gott's done been. Pa paid him with the last o' our chickens. Doc give Ma a tonic. It helped some. She's gonna be all right in time. We'll hold on. Now, tell me your news. Did you give in to Will?"

"Give in? To what?"

Belle chuckled. "Lordy, Byroney, you're as blind as a newborn kitten. Will Atwood's been in love with you from the first day he laid eyes on you. Are you gonna say yes and make the man happy?"

"Are you daft? Will's never said a word to me about love or marriage."

"Tom says Will's gonna ask you first chance he gets!"

"Tom says? What, pray tell, does Tom Jenkins know? And how do you know what Tom knows?" sputtered Byroney.

A flush crept up Belle's neck. "Tom and Will are

friends. Tom's been comin' over to help Pa, in exchange for Pa learnin' him carpentry. We talk right much, me and Tom.''

"I'll bet! Do I sense a Bespoke Party come fall?''

In spite of being tomato red, Belle smiled. "Let's make it a double!''

"Oh, you'll have lots o' company, Belle. Will says Mary and Margaret are courtin' steady. I expect there'll be others,'' By said, fighting a feeling of panic.

Belle frowned. "Does this mean it's Evan you favor?''

"Do I have to favor anyone?'' By exploded. "Evan's no more ready to settle down than I am. He's interested in making money and a name for himself.''

"Simmer down, By,'' Belle said, laughing. "I reckon you'll do as you please, like always. You are the orneriest girl I ever met.''

"Ornery? Me? How?''

"Like Pa's mule, you take delight in being and doing what no one expects. Mind, I love you anyways, just the way you are. You do set tongues a' wagging though.''

"I know,'' By said with a sigh. "I don't set out to be ornery, Belle. What I do seems to fly in the face of some folks.''

"Don't worry on it, By. Most folks love you. Why, I bet the tavern trade's picked up right smart since you began playing and singing most nights.''

"I like working in the tavern. I like people! And I like hearing news of the war firsthand. What's wrong with that?''

"Not a blessed thing. It's just different.''

By didn't need to ask how. She knew. It was unusual for a proper, single lass to work in a tavern. Her Ma nattered at Pa over it, but her Pa won out. Said he needed her.

"Will's a good man," Belle said, breaking into By's thoughts.

"I know he is. You and Tom are wrong though. Will doesn't have me in mind for a wife." She jumped to her feet. "It's gettin' late. I better go."

Belle shook her head. "You're smart 'bout some things, dumb 'bout others, By. You just wait and see."

"I *will* see," By said, fighting down the panicky feeling again. "You sure I can't help out 'round here?"

"We're doin' tolerable well. Thanks for visitin', By."

"My pleasure." By mounted, waved good-bye, and rode off.

The wall-closing-in feeling could not be blown away by Liberty's speed. What if Belle were right? What could she say to Will without hurting his feelings? She *had* to talk with Will. Soon.

Chapter 9

"**A**re you fixing to ask me to wed?" Byroney stood, hands on hips, facing a startled Will. She'd waited for him in the wagon pasture and dragged him off to her willow tree, where they could have some privacy.

Will licked his lips. "What if I was?"

She saw the truth in his naked gaze. Why hadn't she seen it before? She felt the fool. She wouldn't have hurt good, kind Will for the world. "I'm sorry, Will. We're good friends. Hope we always will be. But we're *not* right for each other as man and wif—"

Will grabbed her and kissed her. Hard. Upon the lips.

Surprise was all she felt.

Will released her. "You don't love me," he said flatly.

Unconsciously, she wiped her lips. "Not that way. No. I wish I did."

"Is it Evan?"

"It isn't *anybody*! It may never be anybody! I don't want to be tied to hearth and home!"

"What do you want, Byroney?"

"I don't know," she wailed, clenching her fists at her sides.

"Whatever it is, I hope you find it," Will said. He turned and walked through the curtain of willows.

"Wait, Will! Come back. Can't it be the same as always?" she called, running after him.

Will stopped. His eyes glistened. "Would you pour salt in an open wound, Byroney? Let me heal. We're still friends." Abruptly, he turned and walked away.

Fingering the tiny moon necklace, By watched until he was out of sight among the trees. Then she went back under the willows.

What have I done? Will would make a good husband. He's gentle, kind, thoughtful. A talented artist. He'll take over the Mercantile from his pa one day and provide a good home for wife and children. What more could a girl ask? She sat brooding for a very long time.

Suddenly, footsteps pounded toward her, splashing through the shallow creek. By sat absolutely still, even though she was certain she couldn't be seen.

Nat's freckled face popped through the green fronds. "Wagons comin', By!"

"How many?"

The rest of Nat came into view. "Lots. More'n I can count. Outriders and cattle, too. Saw 'em from Raven Ridge."

"Better go tell Pa. How'd you know where to find me?"

An impish grin split Nat's face. "I've knowed about your hidey-hole for ages. Nothin' gets by ole Eagle Eye."

"Well, I hope you've kept your beak shut, Eagle Eye!"

"Haven't tattled yet, have I?"

"And you better not! Run along now. I'll be along directly."

Sighing, Byroney gathered herself and followed more slowly. If the wagons were at Raven Ridge, she had a good half hour. The Frazers had a set routine worked up now. Even with Uncle Duncan and Andrew away things would run smoothly.

As usual, the wagons made camp in the pasture under Colin and her father's direction. All save one. That wagon slowly and carefully came up the lane toward the Inn.

Ian Frazer rode on ahead of the wagon. "Maggie, Sam Cutter's been bad hurt. I've sent for Dr. Gott. Will you prepare a room?"

"Certainly." With the calm that was her trademark, Margaret swung into action. In no time at all she had the ashen-faced trail guide resting as comfortably as possibe in a room.

"Danged horse stepped in a hole. Fell square on top o' me. Sorry to be sich a bother, Miz Frazer," Sam mumbled.

"Hush, now, Sam. 'Tis no bother. Doctor'll be along shortly. Byroney, fetch me some hot water. Dr. Gott will need it."

He'll need more than hot water, By thought, looking at Sam's mangled leg. Giving Sam an encouraging smile, she ran downstairs.

"How is he, By?" Colin asked as she whizzed past.

"Mama's with him. Where's that doctor?"

"His buggy should be along any minute."

By shook her head in exasperation. The little German doctor refused to ride a horse. It was buggy or foot, no matter how urgent. Still, Abingdon was lucky to have any doctor at all.

When she returned to the sickroom Doc Gott was already bending over Sam. "Can I help?" By asked.

"*Ach,* no! I do not need fainting fräuleins," the doctor said gruffly.

A chuckle errupted from the cot. "No need to worry, Doc. That one's tough as buffalo hide."

75

Byroney flushed with pride, but the doctor was not impressed. "Finish your tisane," he ordered. "Frau Frazer, I will need some strong men."

"I'll send someone. Come along, Byroney."

By opened her mouth to argue, but Sam winked and shook his head. "Don't fret. Be good as new in no time, Missy."

Reluctantly, By followed her mother downstairs.

News of the large wagon train had spread quickly. Already the tavern room was crowded with townspeople seeking news and trade.

Her father met them on the stairs. "How goes it?"

"Too early to tell," Margaret answered. "The doctor says he needs some strong men."

"Aye. James—Robert, come wi' me." Ian bounded up the steps very quickly for such a large man.

There was nothing to do but wait. By kept busy helping Molly serve the patrons, yet keeping one eye on the stairs. When the three rather green-looking men came down she pushed her way through the crowd to her father.

"Doctor says Sam will mend," Ian announced to the room. "Might take a spell though."

Murmurs of sympathy and distress ran through the group. Sam Cutter was well liked by one and all.

"Mr. Frazer, may I have a word?" asked a stranger

"Aye. What can I do for you?"

The dark-haired, blue-eyed man extended his hand. "Liam Mallory, from the wagons. Mr. Cutter said we might rely on you."

"Do my best."

"Most of the wagons are headed for the Watauga and Holston settlements," Mr. Mallory explained. "Sam foresaw no problem for them getting there without his services. My wagon and four others are headed through the Cumberland Gap into Kaintuk."

"You'll no get those wagons through the Gap! 'Tis little more than a footpath."

"We know that now. When we began this journey we were told Virginia had commissioned a road be built."

Byroney snorted in dismay.

"Aye, that they did," Ian agreed. "But near as nothing's been done as yet."

"So we discovered when Sam met us in Beverly," Liam Mallory said wryly. "On his advice, we'll sell off what we can't move by pack mules."

"Makes sense. I see no problem," Ian said.

Mallory's face darkened as he surveyed the collected crowd. "We've been met at every stop by folks willing to buy . . . at less than half o' the value o' our goods! Sam urged us to wait till we got here afore getting skinned."

"Papa's a *fair* man!" Byroney said indignantly.

"That's what Sam said," Mr. Mallory replied, flashing her a dazzling smile. "We counted on you, Mr. Frazer. Yet, 'twill do us no good if we nave no guide through yon Gap."

Ian scratched his head. "I see your problem. Could you no stay here—or in Watauga—until Sam mends?"

"Nay. We have a contract with Colonel Henderson. We must have the land cleared and dwellings up on our homesteads by year's end, else we lose everything! We're willing to endure any hardships to reach a place as fair as the Emerald Isle itself! Can you find us a guide?"

"Hmm . . . My brother could do it, were he here. But he's off wi' my son buying sheep. Don't expect him back for a month or more. I'll speak to Sam soon as he wakes. Mayhap he knows o' someone. We'll do our best, Mr. Mallory."

"Can't ask for more," Liam Mallory said, looking discouraged.

"Who can you get, Pa?" By asked as the man moved away. "All the good guides are spoken for this time o' year."

"Don't know, lass. Go help Molly. She's being run ragged."

"I'll peek in on Sam first."

"He'll be sleeping off the laudanum. You can check by later."

Reluctantly, By went to help Molly. She never stopped moving until Colin relieved her for supper.

"Sam says the onliest guide he can think of—and that's a long shot—is Jericho Jones," her father said in answer to her query. "I aim to ride out to his place in the mountains tomorrow. That is, if I can find it."

"Can I go with you, Papa?" Byroney asked eagerly. "You've been promising to take me riding, hasn't he, Mama?"

"You did promise, Ian."

"Ah weel, a man has no chance against *two* women," her father said, smiling. "Be pleasured to have your company, daughter."

"Thanks, Pa. I'm going to go sit with Sam a spell."

"We'll leave early. You must get a good night's rest. No singing and playing till all hours."

"Yes, Pa." She scampered out the door. This was a chance to face her fear. Somehow the mountains both repelled and called to her. Surely, if she rode safely with someone, the awful nightmares would stop. A true Frazer should have no fears!

Chapter 10

"Haloo, cabin! Jericho Jones, 'tis Ian Frazer, Duncan's brother. May we come up?"

The log cabin nestled among the trees on the hillside was barely visible from the creek where Byroney and her father waited.

Ian Frazer sat quietly, his empty hands and arms in plain view.

Byroney fidgeted. The ride had been long and hot. She longed to dismount and stretch her legs.

"Sit quiet, lass. He's looking us over."

The door of the cabin opened. A small, compact man, dressed in fringed buckskins and fully armed, appeared on the porch. "Come up, Ian Frazer," he boomed in a surprisingly loud, carrying voice.

Byroney was conscious of his eyes following them all the way up the slope. Her father had already warned her that Jericho Jones was a squaw man. He and his Indian wife preferred living far away from prying, condemning eyes. Well, they'd certainly been successful, she thought. This place was about as far away from civilization as you could get. Absolutely beautiful though.

"Howdy, Ian," the man said. "You favor your brother right smart. You be Byroney, I reckon."

"Yes, Mr. Jones."

The man threw back his head, laughing. "I ain't been called mister in donkey years. Hit's just Jericho, ma'am."

"And *I* don't get called ma'am! Just Byroney, or By," she flung back. "Can I get down offa this horse? My legs are cramped, not to mention other parts."

Jericho chuckled. "Get down and set . . . if yer a mind to. What brings you out hyar, Ian?"

Byroney dismounted and stretched luxuriously while her father told of their mission.

"I'm plumb sorry 'bout Sam. You say he'll mend?"

"Aye, with time. Trouble is, he signed on with those folks and can't deliver. It's botherin' him right smart."

Jericho scratched his stubby beard. "Lord knows, I owe Sam a favor or two. I'm caught twixt a rock an' a hard place. My woman's tuk bad sick. I cain't leave."

A small sound of protest issued from the cabin.

Byroney heard it plainly, and so did Jericho.

"I ain't leavin'!" he said firmly. "Come get a drink from the spring, folks. Mayhap we can work sumpin out."

Ian and Byroney followed Jericho to the back of the cabin.

Jericho took a dipper of cold water from the bubbly spring and offered it to Byroney. "Mornin' Flower don't have long on this earth," he confided quietly. "She knows it, and so do I. Don't aim to let her die alone."

"Don't blame you, Jericho. Neither would Sam. I'm sorry for your troubles," Ian said as By passed him the dipper.

"Thankee. She be a good 'oman," Jericho said. Love was etched plainly on his leathery face.

"Is there anything we can do?" By asked, her eyes tearing. "Abingdon has a doctor now. Could we bring him out to see Morning Flower?"

"Bless you, chile, no. Nothin' anyone can do, I'm afeared. Livin's easy. Dyin's hard."

"That it is," Ian agreed. "Sorry we bothered you. We'll be off now."

"Not s' fast, you spikey Scot," Jericho said, smiling. "Reckon I could send Yuncam in my stead. Be easier on him than watching Mornin' Flower pass. Don't think Sam would be displeased."

A cry of pain and a loud thump came from the cabin.

Instantly, Jericho was off. "She oughten t'be outta bed! Tell Sam I'm thinkin' on him."

Quietly, Ian and Byroney remounted and rode off.

By looked over her shoulder. "I wish we could do something!"

"So do I, lass."

"I don't wonder Uncle Duncan thought so highly of Jericho. I liked him, too. Wonder who Yuncam is?"

"Most likely their boy, or some Indian friend," Ian replied, frowning. "Do we take the right or left fork here?"

"Right," By answered without hesitation. "Last turn we made was a left. We go backwards now."

Her father laughed. "Reckon you mind your trail after getting yourself lost."

"You better believe it! I've had nightmares about it," she confessed.

"Then you learnt a good lesson."

It was late in the day when they arrived at the Inn and found another group of weary travelers had come in.

"Praise the Lord! You're back," Molly said. "I could ha' used two o' me."

By hid a grin and set to work. Two of Molly would have displaced quite a few travelers.

She was ready to drop in her tracks by the time Colin packed her off to the cabin. "Go. You're plumb tuckered. Pa and I'll finish up."

For once Byroney didn't argue at being ordered about. She was asleep before her head hit the feather pillow.

She was on the back stoop, washing her face before breakfast, when she felt eyes upon her. Dropping the flour sack, she looked directly into the strangest pair of eyes she'd ever seen ... a piercing grey-blue.

"Howdy." The man stood a trifle over six feet, dressed in deerskins. His flat-brimmed hat sat squarely on his raven black, clubbed hair. Around his waist was a broad sash with a belt ax and scabbard knife. A shot bag and powder horn were slung over his left shoulder. His large brown hands rested easily on the barrel of his grounded long rifle as he endured her careful inspection.

"Howdy," she replied. Her eyes rested longer on his rugged, chiseled face: dark, straight-across eyebrows, high cheekbones, sharp nose, and—surprisingly—a full, generous mouth. . . .

"Jericho sent me. I'm Cam." His voice was quiet and unhurried.

A grin tilted Byroney's lips. "Young Cam?"

A brief nod, his eyes never leaving her face. "Will you take me to Sam?"

"Aye," she answered, but didn't move. The air between them seemed to snap and pop like a pine log fire.

Cam looked away, breaking the spell. "Too early?"

"No. I'll take you. Sam's at the Inn. Wouldn't move in with us. Doc's got him trussed up like a hog for slaughter. I doubt me he slept much last night." She knew she was blathering, but couldn't stop. What was this strange, tingly feeling making her innards jump like water poured on a hot skillet? On she chattered . . .

Cam followed her as silently as a snake moving through summer grass. She had to glance back twice to see if he were with her! Each time a smile twitched the corners of his mouth.

The tavern room was empty as she led Cam upstairs. "Sam's in the first room." She knocked lightly on the door. "Sam, it's Byroney."

"Come on in. I ain't fixin' t' go nowheres," Sam called in a raspy voice.

By opened the door. Sam was flat on his back with one leg suspended in a rope contraption that hung from the rafters. His eyes, though twinkling a welcome, were pain-filled. "Cam's here," she said, standing aside.

"Boy, you've growed another foot!" Sam said.

Cam looked the sling over carefully. "What's this you've growed, Sam?"

Sam chuckled. "Dr. Gott says it'll make them breaks knit faster. Purdy strange, huh?"

Cam shrugged his broad shoulders. "Whatever works."

"How's Morning Flower?"

"Dying. It is her time," Cam answered. "I made my good-byes."

The pain in his voice was so deep Byroney felt the urge to take him in her arms and kiss away the hurt, as she often had done with Nat. To keep from making more of a fool of herself, she said, "I'll fetch breakfast for the both o' you." She practically ran from the room.

"I can't believe your pa would turn white folks over to a half-breed," Molly said, slinging the porridge into two bowls. "Them folks'll never reach Kaintuk with a full head o' hair!"

"Molly! How can you say such? I've never known you to be vengeful," Byroney sputtered.

"You never knowed my sister and her wee ones either! All kilt by Injuns up in Pennsylvania."

83

"I don't think Cam's an Indian," By protested, remembering his light-colored eyes.

"Hmmpt! Half's good as a whole," Molly snapped, shoving the tray at her. "Blood will out."

Stung by Molly's anger, By took the tray upstairs.

Cam had helped Sam freshen up and had propped him on pillows. Byroney could see Sam was hurting something fierce. "Doc left you some medicine for pain, Sam. But you have to eat first. Try to get this down whilst it's hot."

Dutifully, Sam tried to eat the porridge.

Cam ate as silently as he walked. If she hadn't felt his presence so strongly, she wouldn't have known he was in the room.

"Enough," Sam said, refusing two thick slabs of bread. "I'll take Doc's potion now."

After Byroney measured the liquid into water and gave it to Sam, he took a deep breath and said, "Don't think you two've formally met. Byroney Rose Frazer, this be Cameron Jones."

"Howdy," they said in unison. Once again their eyes met and locked. By felt a warmth run clear to her toes. What ailed her?

"Would you fetch your pa?" Sam asked huskily. "Cam's anxious to get under way."

"Sooner gone, sooner back." The fire in his eyes matched the heat she felt.

Byroney shook free of his gaze. "Right. I'll get Pa."

She met her father coming up the stairs. "How's Sam?"

"Hurting. But he ate some. Cameron Jones is waiting for you."

"I know. Molly told me." He went on up the steps, two at a time.

Feeling light-headed, By took the tray back to the cook room. *It's because you haven't eaten,* she told herself. *You're* not *a giddy girl like Mary or Margaret Atwood!* Dipping out a hefty helping of porridge, she sat and ate. She ignored Molly flouncing about, mumbling to herself.

By the time the carts and pack mules began pulling out, Byroney had composed herself. She and her pa stood on the Inn porch and watched as the line of men and beasts slowly snaked down the Wilderness Road.

Cam, mounted on a large bay, held up one hand in farewell.

"He's young," Ian Frazer said, "but Sam vouches for him. Said if anyone could get them through in one piece, it would be Young Cam."

Fear stabbed at Byroney. "Is the way through the Gap that dangerous?"

"Boone's Trail isn't easy, but it's the Indians making it impassable this summer. They don't want more settlers coming in. Best place to stop the flow is along the narrow mountain passes. Whole passels o' people already been lost."

"Why do they go then? Why not stay here? There's plenty of land. They'd be safer."

Her father patted her shoulder. "Safety's not the point, darlin'. Those pushing forward are following a dream. A dream they're willin' to die for. That spirit's why we'll win this war for our independence."

"I hope you're right, Pa. Seems like this war's been going on forever!"

"Don't fash yourself, luv. The road to freedom's long and hard, but we'll no be denied! Matters will turn for the better. You'll see."

Chapter 11

Her father was wrong. Things did not get better. At least, not for Byroney. At church on Sunday morning Mary and Margaret pulled her aside. Very un-Christian anger flushed their faces.

"I hope you're happy, Byroney Frazer," Mary said. "Will's left town!"

"And it's all your fault," added Margaret.

"Will's gone? Where did he go? Why is it my fault?"

"He had a big fight with Papa," Mary said. "He's run off to Charleston to seek his fortune. He told Papa you turned him down, and he couldn't bear to stay where *you* were."

"I never knew what he saw in a wild thing like you anyway!" Margaret said.

"We will never, ever forgive you!" Mary said. "You took our brother away and broke Papa's heart."

Marcus Atwood snapped his fingers and the girls hurried away. But not before Byroney saw the murderous look on Mr. Atwood's face.

"If looks could kill, you'd be a goner," Evan said, coming to stand beside a stunned Byroney. "What did you do to the Atwoods?"

"Will's gone. They blame me," By answered in a hollow voice.

"You probably did Will a favor, getting him out of that house. Don't look so glum, Byroney."

"I'll miss Will. He and Belle were my only good friends," By said, turning to find her family.

"What about me?" Evan asked, walking beside her.

"You, too, Evan . . . when you're around."

"I just might surprise you, Byroney Rose. If the deal I'm working on comes off, I might settle down in Abingdon for good."

"Settle here? I thought you wanted a big city where all the action was."

Evan looked smug. "Better to be a big frog in a small pond, than a little frog in a lake."

By couldn't repress a smile. "Well, if you expect me to kiss you and turn you into a prince, you got another think coming!"

"That's right, my feisty Scottish lass. You keep those lips chaste whilst I'm away," Evan said, chuckling.

"You're leaving, too?"

"On the morrow. First light. Keep well, Byroney."

"You, too."

"Oh, I intend to do just that," Evan said with a laugh. "Remember, I'm like a cat. I always land on my feet."

The small smile Evan provoked was the last on Byroney's face for a while. Sadly, Zelda Crabtree passed on, leaving Belle to care for all her brothers and sisters. Belle was the eldest and would not leave her father to cope with the little ones. By wondered what would happen between Tom and Belle now.

Most of all, she missed Will! Will had always been there for her. They'd shared laughs, hopes, and fears. Now she had no one close by. Mary and Margaret continued to spread their poison. More and more, she felt cut off from the rest of the young people. No one automatically included her in the occasional female gatherings. "Oh, we thought you'd be busy at the Inn," they'd say when word of such a party leaked out. And By would smile, never letting them see the hurt, and say, "I'm sure I was."

She was not alone in her melancholy. A mantle of gloom seeped over the whole settlement that autumn. The harvest was poor. Continental currency was almost worthless. The War was at a frozen standstill in the North. Patriot barns and houses mysteriously burned. The militia tried but never found anyone to punish. It was truly a dreary time. Even the trickle of travelers along the Great Road were glum and disheartened.

Strangely enough, it wasn't the many slights or the War that constantly plagued her thoughts. It was Cameron Jones. He popped into her head at the strangest times! She could recall every feature—from his strange, piercing eyes to his surprisingly tender mouth. Had he gotten the settlers through? Would he come back as he'd promised Sam?

Sam was another worry. Though he was finally up and about, his leg had not mended properly. It was evident he would no longer be able to lead the rigorous life of a freighter/trail guide. At present, he earned his keep by mending tack and tending the animals at the Inn stables.

Byroney spent as much time as possible with the always-cheerful man.

"Don't fash yerself 'bout me," Sam said. "Somethin' will mosey my way. Allus does."

"I'm not worried about you, Sam. You have a home here for as long as you like. In fact, with Duncan leaving again and Andrew besotted with sheep, I don't see how we can do without you."

"Yer pa's already tried that wool pull," Sam said, chuckling. "I thankee, but I got me another notion. Whensomever Cam gits back we'll see do it work."

"Shouldn't Cam be back by now?" By asked, trying to sound casual.

Sam's eyes twinkled. "Any day, I reckon. Hard to put a time to frontier travel. I told him to see them folks settled in good, same as I would. Then he was to collect my wages from Colonel Henderson and head back. Most likely, he stopped in to see 'bout Mornin' Flower."

By shook her head. "I don't think I could leave my dying mother even if Pa asked me to."

"Mornin' Flower ain't Cam's ma. Jericho's not his pa neither. Still, it were a turrible hard thing fer Cam to do," Sam said quietly.

She was stunned. "Not his parents? Who are they? Who is Cam?"

"Them's Cam's privates," Sam said sternly. "It's fer him to tell or not. I already said more'n I oughter. Just don't you think bad on him for doin' what he done."

"I don't think bad of Cam! He just pops into my head all the time," By admitted. "Why is that, Sam?"

"Danged if I know," Sam replied. The twinkle in his eye grew stronger. "Ain't niver happened to me."

By was immediately sorry for her words. "I suppose I'm just curious 'cause he's different," she said primly.

"Like calls to like," Sam said. He continued mending the harness he held.

Exasperated with him and herself, Byroney flounced out of the barn. She did *not* ask him what he meant. She knew. She was falling in love with a man she'd met only once!

Two days later she went to fetch Liberty and found Cameron Jones talking to Sam.

"There you are! Told Cam you'd be along directly," Sam said.

"Howdy, Byroney."

The pine cones went popping again. "You're back," she said stupidly.

"Got them folks through and settled. Brought me my money, too," Sam said into the silence. "Now, if'n you two'd do me a favor, I'd be all set."

By dragged her gaze away from Cam. "What favor?"

"Moses Jackson aims to sell off the livery stable. Take his wife back East. I'm thinkin' on buying him out. Be a job I could handle with this here gimpy leg. What do you think o' that, By?"

Sam's words seemed to come from a long way off. She shook her head to clear it. "Sounds good to me, Sam."

"How can we help?" asked Cam.

Sam chuckled for no apparent reason. "I got my poke hid over t' my place on Little Doe River. If'n ya'll would go fetch it and my belongin's, I'd be most obliged."

She looked at Sam suspiciously. "Why us?"

"Weel, I don't reckon as how anyone else but Cam could find th' place. And, seein' as how I got someone keepin' a eye out, I reckon with you along Cam won't get his head blowed off. Darcy'd be more apt to ast questions first."

"I will go. I do not fear this Darcy," Cam replied.

Was there a hint of challenge in his voice? By held her head high. "I will go, too. If it's all right with Pa."

"Oh, I done checked with Ian," Sam said. "He's agreeable. I warn ya, it's a full day's ride there and back. Think you're up to it, lass?"

"When do we leave?"

"Tommorow. First light?" Cam said.

90

"I'll be ready." She turned on her heel and marched off. Up to it, indeed!

As the first pale fingers of dawn lightened the sky, Byroney slipped out of the cabin, carrying a flour sack filled with food. She carefully picked her way to the barn, intending to be saddled and waiting when Cam arrived.

Cam was already there . . . with his horse and Liberty saddled and a packhorse in tow.

Byroney held out the sack. "Had to get this. Sorry I'm late." Officiously, she began checking Liberty's riggings.

Instead of being offended as she intended, Cam was pleased! "Sam said you was a good rider. Good riders always check their gear." He swung effortlessly up on the big bay.

Byroney mounted. "Sam either talks too much or not enough."

They rode in silence past the sleeping Inn and village. As the sun peeked over the mountains, Cam looked over at her and smiled. "I never heard anyone say Sam Cutter didn't talk more'n enough. He spent a whole winter nursin' Jericho and never told the same tale twice, according to Jericho."

"Oh, he's good at tales," By conceded. "Just not much on information."

"He can be closemouthed. When I tried to find out more about you last night, you'd thought he had lockjaw!"

She giggled. "Same about you."

"Reckon we best satisfy our own curiosity?"

"Looks like the only way we'll ever know."

"Ladies first," Cam said. "Start at the beginning."

"I was born in Scotland . . ." Byroney began. Cam was a good listener. He asked questions, prying feelings out of her she didn't know she had. Even the lingering hurt over her "ghost" Indians tumbled out.

"This Captain Eggleston did not know the mountains," Cam said disdainfully. "The Indians you saw were at Sacred Rocks, a frequent stop on Warrior Path. Any scout worth his salt knows that. They only had to listen to your description."

"Well, they didn't listen. Everyone thought I was a liar or a show-off. Pa was furious with me for breaking my word."

"One's word is sacred. It should not be broken."

"I know that! I didn't mean to. I was angry and hurt over something else. I acted without thinking."

"Out here that could get you killed," Cam said, smiling but serious.

"It almost did." She turned to him. "Now, it's your turn."

"My folks, like Jericho, was born in Wales. In a coal mining village. The British company that owned the mines shipped a whole passel o' miners over t' Pennsylvania to mine coal. They was supposed to work out their freedom, like your folks. But, due to slick company dealing, they never had no hope o' being free. Finally, a bunch o' them just up and left. My Ma and Pa—Glyds and Cameron Jones—and our cousin Jericho was amongst the deserters. They fled into the wilderness, built a village, and took care o' themselves. I was borned there."

"In Pennsylvania?"

"Don't rightly know. I was only 'bout four when a Shawnee war party swooped down and killed everybody but me and two other boys. Jericho was out huntin', and when he come back all he found was burnt cabins, crops, and scalped bodies. Drove him near mad, he said."

"What did the Indians do with you?"

"Raised me like one o' their own."

"What about the other boys?"

"Traded off to other tribes. I never saw another white face till Jericho rode in one day when I was 'bout nine. Somehow he recognized me. Said I looked just like my Pa. Anyhow, he haggled with Black Fox for me and a squaw captured on a recent raid. Said he wanted a wife and family."

"Goodness! I bet you were happy."

"Happy? I was madder'n a winter-woke bear. I'd come to love the Beaver Clan like they was my own family. How could they trade me for a few bolts o' cloth, some beads, and shot? Fact was, I'd forgot I was white. Couldn't speak a word o' English."

"You do very well now."

"Jericho teached me and Morning Flower. Wish he'd knowed how to read. I pure-T would like to learn me that."

"I could teach you," By said shyly. "Ma taught all of us our letters and numbers. We still have the books. Nat's almost finished with them."

"I'd be much obliged," Cam said, smiling so brightly it made her heart do funny things. "What can I learn you in return?"

"You could teach me to read signs like you been doing for the last hour," By said, laughing. "Your eyes are never still. You never falter at a fork in the trail. You act like you got a map in your head."

"The Shawnee and Jericho learned me. I'd be proud to pass it along."

"Start now."

So for the next hour or two Cam instructed her in woodsmanship. Byroney listened as carefully as she could, though admittedly she was distracted by how easily he sat his horse, and by how mellow and sure his voice flowed from his lips. But it was his eyes that spoke louder than any words. His glances, however brief, caressed her. They spoke of a desire that matched her own. It was like flint sparks striking tinder every time their eyes met.

"We're about t' Sam's," he announced, reining. "This here is Little Doe. Cabin should be along here somewheres."

By saw nothing but trees on a gentle hillside as they splashed across the shallow river. "Looks like Sam's friend isn't on duty."

"Don't see any sign o' life," Cam agreed, his eyes scanning the area. "There's the cabin."

"Where? I don't see anything."

Cam pointed to a spot in the hillside.

Byroney focused her eyes in that direction. Suddenly, she saw it. The cabin was so cleverly built you could pass a few yards from it and never notice it.

"I'll go in first," Cam said, as they dismounted. "Might be a varmint has took up residence whilst Sam's away."

"Hold it right thar. Don't twitch nary a muscle!"

Chapter 12

The command came from the deep woods. Cam and Byroney froze.

A man, as straight and slender as the pine he stepped from behind, appeared. His rifle was aimed at Cam's heart. "Who be you?"

Byroney stepped in front of Cam, shaking her hair loose from under her hat. "Howdy, Darcy. I'm Byroney Frazer. This is Cameron Jones."

The man squinted at them. "Ya be th' innkeeper's daughter?"

"One and the same. Sam had a bad accident. He's been staying at the Inn whilst his leg mends. He sent us to fetch his belongings."

The rifle lowered. "Heard you was a redhead. How's Sam doin'?"

Cam eased By aside. "His leg's mended, but he won't be trail riding no more. Has a mind t' buy the livery stable in Wolf Hills."

"Sorry t' hyar o' Sam's troubles," Darcy replied, relaxing somewhat. "Sam allus was good with horse-flesh. Reckon he'll do right well. Kin I hep ye?"

"We'd 'preciate your help," Cam said, walking

95

slowly forward. "Sam said what all he didn't need was yourn, could you use it."

Darcy leaned his rifle against a tree. "That be right generous o' Sam."

While Darcy and Cam rummaged through the tiny cabin, Byroney excused herself modestly. She went toward the privy, but veered to a nearby stack of logs. She found the metal box just where Sam said it would be, and slipped it into her saddlebags before joining the men.

It didn't take long to clear the cabin. By insisted Darcy share their food before they packed out.

"Them's the best biscuits I ever et!" Darcy said, picking crumbs from his shirt. "What was it you called 'em?"

"Scones. They're Scottish biscuits. I made them myself."

"Scones." Darcy rolled the word around in his mouth several times. "Whatsomever. They's good."

"You come over to Abingdon to visit Sam and I'll bake you some, fresh and hot," By offered.

As they rode off a smile played around Cam's lips.

"Do I amuse you, Cameron Jones?" she asked rather huffily.

Cam looked at her and shook his head. "If you were Indian, your name would be Red Fox Woman."

Self-consciously, By touched her russet hair. "Because of this?"

"Partly. But mostly because you are quick and cunning like Sister Fox."

"I am?"

"You are. Without thinking, you distracted Darcy and shielded me, giving me time to draw my knife."

By was pleased he'd understood her actions. "Most of the time I get scolded for acting without thinking."

"But you were thinking! Instincts are important in

the wilderness. The Wolf and the Fox work well together.''

''Was Wolf your Indian name?'' she asked as a wave of pleasure washed over her.

Cam nodded. ''White Wolf. Two Knife, my Indian father, said I howled like a wolf when I was young and displeased.''

She giggled at the thought of a young Cam howling with displeasure.

Cam looked embarrassed. ''Later it was because of my hearing. I seemed to be able to hear sounds a long way off. I guess I've lost that or that crafty dodger wouldn't a sneaked up on us. I never heard a thing. Suppose my mind was elsewhere. Jericho would not be happy wi' me.''

''I reckon I was chattering so much neither o' us would have heard thunder,'' By said, by way of apology.

''That's dangerous out here,'' Cam said. ''Sam and your pa would skin me alive had anything happened to you.''

''Well, nothing did! We got what we came for and made a new friend.''

Cam laughed. ''Reckon I'd partner with you any day.''

''Why, thankee kindly, sir. Same here.'' She spoke lightly, but her heart was doing strange flip-flops.

Talk flowed between them like a river. She felt as if she'd known him forever. Cam told her of his years with the Shawnee and with Jericho. When he spoke of the vast lands that lay beyond the mountains it made her wish to see it all for herself.

''We're home already,'' By said in surprise as they turned into the Inn lane at dusk.

''Seemed a mite shorter comin' back,'' Cam said. ''I

never jawed so much in my whole life. Right pleasurable.''

"Speaking of pleasure, there's a sociable at Camden Mill tomorrow night. Would you care to come?''

"With you?''

"With the family. Pa usually fiddles.'' She was glad the fading light hid her warming face. She was being right bold!

"I never been to a sociable,'' Cam confessed.

"Oh, there's music, dancing, and eating. You'd like it, Cam.''

He hesitated. "You sure you want me to come?''

"Please, Cam. Come to the house after supper. We'll go together.''

Sam hobbled out of the barn. "Y'all made good time. Any trouble?''

By glanced at Cam and smiled. "Not a speck. Darcy sends his regards.'' She dismounted and took out the tin. "Here's your poke, Sam.''

"Thankee. Me and Cam'll look after the horses. You run on. Your ma's a mite worrit.''

"Thanks.'' She sailed down to the cabin as if on wings. It had been a purely satisfying day!

"I saw you ride in,'' her ma said. "I've kept your supper warm. Sit and eat.''

Byroney knew that tone. Her ma was riled over something. She helped herself from the stewpot and settled at the table. In between bites, she related her day.

Margaret Frazer sat by the fire, mending, without comment.

"It was a grand day!'' By said defiantly. "Why are you not happy with me?''

"It's not you. I am provoked wi' your father.''

"What's Pa done?''

"He should no ha' let you ride off all day wi' a stranger! Particularly, that one.''

"What's wrong with Cam?"

"Folks say he's a half-breed."

"Well, he isn't! And what if he was? He's a fine person . . . gentle, caring, smart, and fun to be with."

"Don't get that Frazer dander up wi' me, young lady. I'm telling you what folks *think*. And I'm doing it for your own good. Your pa should ha' had better sense."

Byroney pushed away from the table. "I don't care what folks say or think! And, what's more, I've invited Cam to the sociable tomorrow night."

Margaret Frazer's face softened. "Oh, Byroney, I didna miss the look on your face. I've been there meself. You're letting yerself open to a load o' grief, child."

"I am *not* a child!" Without another word, she picked up her plate and stormed out to the back stoop to wash it and herself before changing clothes and going to the tavern.

The mill floor had been swept clean. Oil lamps hung from every post. Music and laughter filled the air. Dancers occupied center floor, whilst others mingled and ate from the loaded tables along the sides. In spite of the lean harvest, folks were bent on celebrating.

There was a noticeable lull in conversation when Byroney and Cam entered beside her father and Andrew.

"Come take my spot," Abel Anderson called from the bale of hay he was perched on. "My catgut's 'bout howled out."

"Mine's apt to be worse," Ian answered modestly.

Andrew made a beeline for Demity.

That left By and Cam standing alone. "Come on, Cam. I'll introduce you around," By said, taking his arm.

Their reception was polite but cool.

"Where's yer ma?" Mrs. Craig asked.

"Nat came down with a cold. She had to stay t' home. Edith looks mighty pretty tonight."

"Thankee," Mrs. Craig replied and turned aside.

It happened over and over. Folks turned away or barely spoke.

Cam was calm and politeness itself.

Byroney was getting madder by the minute. "Want to dance this set, Cam?"

"I don't know how to dance, Byroney."

"Oh, it's easy. Just do what everyone else does and keep time to the music."

"Maybe they'll play a war dance," someone behind them muttered. "Bet he could do that."

Byroney whirled to see who'd been so rude. A solid knot of unfriendly faces met her glare. She started into their middle, but a gentle pressure on her arm restrained her.

"Let it lay," Cam said softly.

With a great effort, Byroney swallowed her anger. "Let's get out of here." She put her arm through Cam's and, head high, made her way to the door.

"Where to?" Cam asked once they were out in the cool, crisp air.

"Home! I can't abide another minute of those ... those ..."

"Easy," Cam said. He stroked her hair as if he were gentling a fractious horse. "What did you expect, Byroney Rose?"

"I expected manners from these good Christian people!" she exploded. "They're judging you without knowing you. They don't know what the Indians did to you! You have more cause to hate Indians than they do."

Cam kept pace with her angry strides. "I don't hate Indians, Byroney."

She stopped abruptly in the middle of the road. "You don't?"

"No. This was their land long afore the white man came. We came in large numbers, cleared their forest, killed their game, and drove them out o' their homes. We made treaties and broke 'em whenever it suited us. Would you not be angry if someone did that to you and your family?"

"Aye. I would."

"Would you fight to hold and protect your own?"

"Yes!"

"How?"

"Any way I could."

"Then you are no different from the Indians. They use any means possible to protect their homes and families. I cannot hate them for that. The Beaver Clan treated me well."

Cam's words gave her much to think on. She walked silently for a few minutes. "Reckon I never looked at Indians that way, Cam," she said slowly. "Never thought of them as people. Only savages who killed, scalped, and burned. I never bothered to ask why."

"You are not alone. You saw that tonight."

"But you're a white man!"

"Who has lived with Indians. Who perhaps understands them. Your friends suspicion that. With good reason. They have lost many in Indian raids."

Byroney stopped at the foot of the cabin steps. Cam's finely chisled face was easy to see by the light of the harvest moon. "You knew this would happen, didn't you?"

"Thought it might."

"Why didn't you say something?"

"Jericho says we learn more by making our mistakes than having others tell us what's wrong," Cam answered simply.

"Pah! It may be true of some things, not all. Besides, once folks get to know you they'll think differently."

"I do not have time. I go tomorrow."

By felt as if someone had stabbed her heart. "Where? Why?"

Cam took her small hands in his big ones. "When Morning Flower died Jericho took the Sorrow Trail. It must be walked alone. But he left sign telling where he would be, did I care to join him for the long hunt. I go."

"I . . . I thought you'd stay . . . to get Sam settled in."

"Sam does not need me."

I do, By thought. *We've only begun to get acquainted. I need to know you better—understand this feeling . . .*

"I *must* go, Byroney. It is best."

"Will you come back? To Wolf Hills, I mean."

"I will come in spring." He bent and brushed his lips across hers. "Keep safe and well." He let go of her hands and slipped silently into the shadows.

A small moan escaped Byroney's lips. It felt as if a part of her had been ripped out. How could that be? She'd only known Cam such a short time. Did he feel the same? The feathery kiss said something . . . what, she wasn't sure. Sighing, she turned and stumbled up the steps.

"Who's there?" Margaret Frazer called.

"Me." By made her way inside.

A compassionate look flitted across her mother's face, but she said nothing.

By hung up her shawl and came to sit by the fire. "You knew what would happen, didn't you?" she asked bitterly.

"I had my suspicions."

"Well, you were right. People were mean and rude.

102

I shouldn't have invited Cam until folks got to know him."

"It gives me no pleasure to be right, By. Give folks time to know Cam and his story."

"They won't have the opportunity. Cam's gone." She stared into the fire. "I don't understand people, Mama. Not even myself."

" 'Tis a lifetime task. You've just begun. Don't be so impatient."

"It's hard, Mama! Why does it have to be so hard?" Oddly, Cam's kiss lingered on her lips. It wasn't like Will's kiss. Why? "Mama, do you think I'm strange?"

"Och, no! Why do you ask such a question?"

By sighed. She couldn't tell her ma about the kiss. That was too personal. She approached another problem that bothered her. "I don't know. All my friends are either bespoke or married. Belle plans to marry Tom after Christmas. Mary told me—gleefully—that Will has wed a Charleston girl. I don't even have a beau."

"That's your own choice."

"I know! I'm not ready to settle down to hearth, home, and children. There's so much more I'm interested in. Why do I feel this way when other girls don't?"

"Perhaps you haven't met your soul mate yet," her mother replied.

"How will I know my soul mate?"

A dreamy expression softened her mother's face. "Oh, you'll know. Both o' you will. 'Tis worth waiting for, Byroney luv."

Cam's kiss tingled her lips, then Will's face floated before her. "What if you love someone and he or she doesn't love you back?"

"Then you weren't soul mates. Not right for each other. 'Tis best not to wed."

"This is too complicated!" By stormed. "Why do I need a soul mate anyway? I do very well on my own."

"God had Noah bring the animals in two by two," her mother replied, smiling.

"Well, I'm not expecting a flood anytime soon! Perhaps it is my lot to go through life alone." She rose and kissed her mother's cheek. "I'll check on Nat and then turn in. Thinking makes me tired."

Chapter 13

"This winter started out bad and has got worser an' worser!" The half-frozen man stood by the blazing fire, shaking like a wet dog. The smell of wet wool permeated the tavern.

"Here, drink this," By said, handing him a mug of hot cider. "It'll warm your insides."

" 'Pears like it's a gonner last ferever," the man said glumly.

She, too, thought this winter of '78–'79 would never end. People lost toes, fingers, and even their lives in the bitter cold. Hunting was impossible for man and beast. Wolves and wildcats prowled ever closer to the settlement, attacking anything helpless. Andrew's flock grew smaller day by day. Everybody had the dismals.

"Good thing yore road was clear. Don't think I'd a lasted another mile."

"My lads do a good job wi' that," Ian said proudly. "What use is a Inn if you can't get to it?"

By smiled to herself as she went to fetch more cider. She rather thought the men of Abingdon would have found a way to the tavern if they'd had ten-foot drifts! Wolf Hills had become the gathering place this dark, frigid winter. Her pa was a canny Scot as well as a Patriot!

"Lucky for me," she said as she plunged a hot iron into another mug of cider. Because all her friends were married and because of Mary and Margaret Atwood's continued spite, she spent most of her time helping in the tavern, the best part being in the evening, when she played the harp or sang duets with Peter whilst her Pa fiddled. Kept other folks' spirits up, too.

"Are you comin' wi' the mull, lass?"

"On my way, Pa."

As she handed the steaming cup to the traveler, another voice called, "Make one for me, Byroney."

By smiled at one of their most frequent visitors. "Coming up, Evan. Anyone else?"

After delivering the orders, she joined Evan at his usual table. "So, Mr. Finder, did you bring me what I asked you to search for?"

Evan frowned. "What, By? I can't remember you asking aught of me."

"Some finder you are! I asked for spring!"

"It's on its way, I promise. I do bring good news though."

"What? We could use a piece o' good news."

"Nothing about the war, my little Patriot. All that's frozen in. This is personal. I signed the papers yesterday for one hundred acres along Pumpkin Creek! It's all mine."

Evan had returned before the second blizzard, flush with money and plans. Stubborn old man Tipton had been a thorn in his side. "Mr. Tipton sold! That's wonderful, Evan."

Evan leaned back with a satisfied smile. "That isn't even the best part, By. I aim to build a two-story, brick house on Pumpkin Creek."

"Brick? Now where would you be getting brick, Evan?"

"I'll make them! Your're looking at the proprietor of Kincaid Brickworks. Soon as thaw sets in, I'll go hire me some masons and brickmakers. The clay on the far end o' my property is perfect for making brick. Everybody who's anybody is going to want a warm, redbrick home, instead of these log ones."

"Why a two-story house? Pretty fancy for a traveling man like you, isn't it?"

Evan's eyes twinkled. "My traveling days are almost over, By. I aim to settle here. I'll fill the house with wife and children. We'll be one of Abingdon's leading families. Perhaps even a noteworthy Virginia family."

"Are you forgetting there's a war on?"

"It can't last forever. I believe in being prepared. With your help, of course."

"My help?"

Taking her hand, Evan said, "By, you know men build houses, but they're never good at planning what goes inside. You could do that for me, couldn't you?"

She retrieved her hand. "I suppose. You have anyone in mind for a wife?"

"Could be," Evan replied, giving her a look that made her blush.

"I'd best get back to work." By rose from the bench and hurried off amid laughter from the nearby tables. Lord-a-mighty! One couldn't have a private talk in this place!

Everyone assumed they were a courting couple. She liked Evan well enough, so let them think what they pleased. It was fun planning the grand house. Evan was well-thought of in Abingdon. Why, there'd even been talk of sending him to Williamsburg to represent the town's interest. Ma and Pa seemed to like him, too. He was generous, often bringing her little presents . . . ª

107

comb for her hair, ribbons, a lace handkerchief. Generous with his time, too. Saying he had no family responsiblities yet, he often volunteered to take messages for Colonel Campbell or ride out to check on outlying farms. Still, everyone was wrong. There was no fire between them. Not like with Cam. Did fire matter? It did to her. But at least she had someone to talk and laugh with this long, dreary winter.

So she spent many hours with Evan, drawing and discarding house plans. While at night, in her dreams, she wandered the Wilderness with Cam. Sometimes she awoke aching with longing for the sight of his chiseled face . . . his piercing blue-grey eyes . . . his soft lips. . . .

Spring, when it came, was glorious. Every tree and plant burst into bloom. The air was so heavily perfumed you could taste the sweetness when you breathed.

Hearts and spirits lifted. Folks went around with smiles on their faces and in their voices. Gardens were plowed. Seeds planted. Hope sprang up as thick as the flowers.

"Have you heard aught about Cam?" By asked Sam one day at his flourishing livery stable.

"Nary a word. Mayhaps him and Jericho went further than afore. Don't fret. Them two's all right."

"I'm *not* fretting. Just curious."

Sam scratched his head. "Me, I'm curious, too."

"About what"

" 'Bout why you be stewin' over Cam. Way I hear it, you got another interest."

By felt her face warming. "Since when do you listen to gossip, Sam Cutter?"

"I seen you with my own eyes, head t' head with that Kincaid feller."

"So? What's wrong with helping a friend?" By asked, tossing her head.

"Nuthin'. But I'd go careful, was I you," Sam warned.

"Well, you're not me," By said. She kicked Liberty abruptly and galloped off.

Her emotions in a swivet, she rode out of town. What was Sam nattering about? She knew Sam and Evan had had a spat over some business dealings. Was that it? Did he expect her to wait around for Cam to turn up? She was, wasn't she? Why? Did she love Cam or Evan? And how was she supposed to tell? She'd never been in love before! There were no answers to be found on her long ride. Her inner turmoil gave her an attack of the dismals.

"What have you done with my jolly niece?" Duncan demanded when he returned the next week. He held By at arm's length. "You don't look like my Byroney. Go fetch her this instant!"

"I suppose I've just grown up, Uncle Duncan," she replied, trying to give him her old smile. "I'm sure folks will be happy to tell you of my contrary ways."

"They best talk fast. I'm back to Kaintuk soon as I sell my booty. Found a beautiful woman who's fool enough to wed me."

Some of the lost joy came back to Byroney's voice. "Uncle Duncan, that's fair wonderful! Why didn't you bring her with you? Marry her here?"

"She's a young thing and will not leave her mither," warbled Duncan. "I best hie me back afore Mary changes her mind."

A week later he'd sold his furs, settled up with Ian, and was happily on his way. "Don't look so sad, By. Be happy for me," Duncan said, hugging her.

"I am happy for you. I wish we'd had more time to talk. I'll miss you, even your teasing."

"Come visit me and I'll tease you to kingdom come. You'll love Mary. She's a spitfire, like you."

"You *should* bring your bride to meet your family," Ian said. "We'd welcome her into the clan."

"Oh, I'll do that for certain. Farewell, till then." Duncan rode out, leading pack mules loaded with wedding gifts from the Frazers.

By felt an acute sense of loss. For some reason she'd felt she could talk to her uncle about Cam and Evan. There was no one else she felt free with. Every time Cam's name was mentioned her mother's face grew still and quiet. Her father and brothers were of no use, and Belle had her hands more than full. Other folks seemed waiting for her to announce a Bespoke Party—for her and Evan! It was widely assumed that the "unplucked Rose" would finally settle down and become a proper Abingdon lady. It was driving her mad!

Two days after her uncle departed, she opened the cabin door and saw Cam coming up the steps! Forgetting all modesty, she flew at him, pelting him with questions. "Where've you been? What took so long? Did you find Jericho?"

A beautiful smile lit his weary face. "Whoa! One at a time. Can we set? I'm plumb tuckered."

"Over here under the oak. We can talk privately here. Have you eaten?"

"Vittles later. I can't stay long, Byroney."

"You just got here!"

"I know," he replied, rubbing a hand over his tired eyes. "Let me answer your questions whilst I can. I found Jericho. We hunted way-far west. Lordy, By, this country's a sight to behold. I kept thinkin' on you ... how you'd love it. Anywise, we had good fortune. Come back to the Holston to raft our hides downriver. Run into Colonel John Sevier. Him and Jericho's friends from way back. Colonel Sevier, he ast us if we'd do him a favor. We did."

"What favor?"

"Sevier got wind o' a secret powwow about to take place. War parties from five tribes was to jine up agin the settlements. He wanted me and Jericho to find these Indians and try to talk sense into 'em afore they got together to attack."

"Did you?"

Cam nodded. "Jericho's powerful persuasive. Him and Sevier got a heap o' them to turn back. Wadn't easy. The British are supplying 'em with guns and powder. Don't know fer how long we can stop 'em."

"We?"

Cam seemed to ignore her question. He took her hands and looked directly into her eyes. "Did I come t' mind whilst I was gone?"

The familiar fiery current ran through her. "You did."

"I carried you in my heart every day," he said quietly. "Even when Jericho told me something awful, I couldn't chase you away. It's why I come back."

Her heart was pounding so hard she thought surely it would come through her ribs. "What did Jericho tell you?"

"You 'member when I told you my ma and pa was indentured to the British mining company?"

By nodded. "What has that to do with you?"

"Under British law any offspring o' theirn is indentured, too. Jericho *and* me got a bounty on us."

"But you weren't born in the mining camp!"

"No. Neither was them other two boys. The Llewellyn Company found them and took them right back to work in the mines."

"Children? That's terrible. Why did they want children?" By asked, outraged.

"Younguns can crawl in spaces a full-growed man cain't. Anywise, I'm not a free man long as we're under British rule. Add that to my livin' Indian, and you got two good reasons to shy away from me. I think we both best forget.''

"Can you do that?'' By asked, knowing suddenly she could not. In spite of everything he'd told her, she knew for certain he was the one man for her. Cameron Jones had a combination of Will's kind heart, Evan's drive, Uncle Duncan's wanderlust, and her father's sense of honor. She would not let that honor stand in her way.

Cam's face looked like chiseled stone. "I aim to try. Me and Jericho has signed up with Colonel Sevier. Hope to help win this war and be free. I wouldn't speak to yer Pa lest I was a free man. Won't ast you to wait neither.''

By grabbed his face with both hands and kissed him full on the mouth. "You have no say in the matter, Cam Jones. I'll wait if I've a mind to,'' she said when she finally broke away.

Cam kept her hugged to him. She could feel his heart thumping in rhythm with her own. "Reckon neither one o' us got a choice,'' he said huskily.

For several minutes they sat intertwined. Byroney had never felt so safe, so happy. For better or for worse, she'd cast her lot with Cam. They were tied to each other as securely as any preacher's knot could tie them.

Sighing deeply, Cam let her go. "I'd best be on my way.''

"When will you be back?''

"I'll come often as I can. Might be quite a spell. Sevier has work fer us. You can still change your mind, Byroney.''

"I'll be here whenever you come—be it tomorrow or a year.''

Smiling, Cam rose, took her in his arms, and kissed her long and hard. "I won't hold you to that, but I will be back.'' Then as silently as a puff of smoke on the wind, he disappeared into the trees.

Weak-kneed and dizzy, she turned to go back inside the cabin.

Her mother stood silently on the porch. "I see you've made your choice," she said, as Byroney floated up the steps.

"Yes, Ma."

Her mother followed her inside. "Mind telling me how you decided?"

"Don't know exactly. Oh, Ma, the first time I laid eyes on him it was like I'd been struck by a lightning bolt. I went numb, then frazzled." By paused, searching for words. "It . . . it's like a part o' me is missing when Cam's not around. Does any o' this make sense?"

"Love never makes sense," Margaret Frazer replied wryly. "It 'pears like you've found your soul mate though. Has Cam spoke to your pa?"

By shook her head. She almost blurted out Cam's secret, but thought better of it. "Cam and Jericho have joined Sevier's Overmountain men. Till the War's won, Cam won't speak to Pa."

"You're willing to wait unspoken for?"

By drew herself up to her full height. "Aye! I'll have Cameron Jones for a husband or no husband at all." Her shoulders sagged. "Be happy for me, Mama."

Her mother smiled ruefully. "I am happy, By. Just a mite selfish. You're my only daughter. Reckon I wanted you to marry a local and settle close by."

Relief flooded By's face. Her ma didn't dislike Cam! "We might settle here once this war's over."

Margaret shook her head. "No, Byroney, you and Cam have wild, seeking hearts. You aren't ready to settle yet. You'll leave this place and family. The Wilderness Road doesn't end here for you."

"How can you know that, Mama? Are you fey?" By asked, smiling.

"No, I'm not fey. I just know you. You'll go, mark my words."

In two steps By was across the space dividing them. She hugged her mother fiercely. "Don't be sad, Mama. I won't be gone for a while yet."

Unused to such demonstrations, Margaret Frazer was flustered. "It does seem as if this war will never end," she said, straightening her apron.

"I wish I could do something besides sit and wait!"

"Waiting's always been a woman's lot, Byroney. Best get used to it."

"It isn't fair! Who made that rule? A man, I'll wager. Women want freedom as much as men. We should be able to fight for it!"

"Don't talk foolishness, By. And, for heaven's sake, promise me you won't *do* anything foolish!"

"I'm past that now, Ma. Haven't I behaved proper lately?"

"Aye, that you have. I hope you'll continue that behavior when you tell Evan o' your decision."

By sobered immediately. "I dread doing that, Ma."

"You must. The sooner, the better."

Chewing on her lower lip, By said, "I can't tell him about Cam, Mama. Cam hasn't spoken to Pa. What will I tell Evan?"

"The truth," her mother answered. "Tell Evan you can't live up to his and other folks' expectations though you've tried."

"The truth is, Mama, Evan never asked me to wed. Mayhap he won't be too unhappy."

"Don't count on it. Evan's a proud, ambitious man, Byroney. Do it soon, for both your sakes."

"I will," By promised with a sigh.

True to her word, she pulled Evan aside that very evening. "I'm taking a break. Would you care to stroll with me down the lane?"

"My pleasure."

Knowing glances and smiles followed them out the door.

"Beautiful night," Evan said.

"Yes," By agreed, swallowing hard. All afternoon she'd thought over what she would say. Now the words were stuck in her throat. "Uh, Evan, did you note the looks we got as we went out?"

"You always attract looks, Byroney," he said gallantly.

"They bother me, Evan. More and more, folks seem to think we're bespoken or about to be. I know you've noticed."

"And if I have?"

"It isn't fair! Folks are pushing us together when we don't belong," By said angrily. "We aren't suited to each other, Evan."

"We aren't? I thought you enjoyed my company."

"I do. We're friends. Planning the house with you has been fun. But I don't love you."

"Are you certain?" he asked, trying to take her in his arms.

Byroney pushed him away. "Don't be daft, Evan. We aren't suited. I don't give a fig about fine houses and high positions. You need a wife who shares your dreams."

"I thought you did."

"No, you didn't. You never asked me to wed. In your heart you knew we weren't fated to be man and wife. Think on it. You'll see I'm right."

He walked in silence beside her for a few minutes. "Perhaps you are. What do we do now? Can I still come to the tavern?" he asked in a little boy voice.

"Don't be silly! Of course you can. We're still friends. Don't be sad about this, Evan, please."

"Sad? I am mortally wounded," he cried, clutching his chest dramatically.

"Evan, be serious."

"I am serious," he said, playfully tweaking her nose. "You have taken one of my nine lives. Now I have only eight left."

"Then you will survive. Let's go back and begin squashing the rumors of our undying love," By said, laughing.

"Shall we stage a lovers' quarrel?"

"No, just get busy finding yourself a suitable wife to carry out your plans."

"There may be changes, but I always carry out my plans, Byroney. Lead on."

She took his arm and they headed back to the Inn. She was relieved he'd taken it so well . . . a little miffed, too. If he were crushed by her rejection, he certainly wasn't showing it!

Chapter 14

"**P**atience is a virture," extolled Pastor Dumfrey.

By squirmed on the hard pew. *Then I am not virtuous,* she thought. *I've lost what little patience I ever had. I want this war done! I want Cam with me all the time, not these short, infrequent visits he's paid this past year now!* Cam refused to compromise her by letting folks know of their relationship. "Time enough for that, By," he said, "when I can openly speak to your pa. What if I was killed or, God forbid, we lose this war? You'd be a marked woman was you married to me."

"I don't care," she'd replied. "We could snatch a few moments of happiness together. Nothing's certain in this life." Oddly enough, she who had never wanted to wed now yearned for marriage with an almost-physical ache.

"I'm not willin' to settle for snatches," Cam said, kissing her lightly. And that was his final word. Nothing could sway him. She longed for Cam's arms always around her . . . that fire betwixt them. . . .

A glance from her mother made her blush. She settled back and tried to concentrate on the preacher's words, but she'd lost the thread of his sermon. Resolutely, she turned her thoughts to the state of the War. . . .

The "easily quelled rabble unrest," as British General Clinton called their war, was in its sixth year this fall of 1780. The Patriots would not give way! Why, at this time last year the English held only a post on Penobscot River, New York City, and the colony of Georgia. Bested in the North, General Clinton had turned his forces to the South. Though fighting had raged in South Carolina for months, he hadn't found the South easy. Many of the mountain men had gone to aid their neighbors from time to time. She could name quite a few. . . .

Byroney was so deeply in her thoughts that Nat had to poke her in the ribs when time came to stand for the last hymn.

"Tilly Jackson's invited me to have dinner," Colin said, blushing furiously. "Is that all right with you, Ma?"

"Of course. Run along. Mind your manners."

"Yes, ma'am."

"Me and Demity are eating with her folks today," Andrew reminded. He held Demity's arm proudly. They'd been married almost a year now. Demity was expecting come spring.

Outside on the church lawn people gathered into distinct age and interest groups, passing news and gossip. As usual, By fit nowhere. She was too young for her parents' friends, too old for the younguns, and out of place with the young married folks with families. Smiling as if it didn't matter, she wandered from group to group, chatting with everyone.

Agnes Moffat, née Craig, thrust one of her twins into By's arms. "Help me out here, Byroney, whilst I wipe Jorden's spit-up."

"This is Joshua, I take it."

"Uh-huh. He's not as colicky as Jorden. Law me, if I'd a known what a trial these two would be, I'd a been more like you."

"Like me?"

"Unmarried and fancy-free," Agnes said. "Reckon I didn't know when I was well off. I work from sunup to sundown, and stay up most nights with these two."

By bit back her hurt and anger. "I work pretty hard at the Inn, Agnes."

Agnes took Joshua back. "At least you get a full night's sleep onct in a while. If it's not these two pesterin' me, it's James." Face flushing, she waddled away with her bairns.

"I suppose there are some advantages in being a tavern wench," Margaret Atwood Colier murmured just loud enough for By to hear.

By whirled to face her tormentor and felt an impatient tug on her sleeve. "Come on, By," Nat said. "Ma's waiting for us in the carriage."

By shook free and smiled. "Reckon if I was the daughter of a profiteer I'd be a mite careful calling names."

Margaret blushed furiously. Since Will's departure, Marcus Atwood was notorious for his skinflint money dealings with travelers. Even the Abingdon residents avoided trading with him whenever possible.

"Come on," Nat urged, almost dragging her away. When he was out of earshot, he said fiercely, "Pay her no heed, By. Everybody knows Trot Colier married Margaret for her pa's money."

"Margaret was mean-spirited long before she wed!" By snapped. In fact, there were a lot worse names she could have called Marcus Atwood. He was still her favorite choice for the elusive Tory traitor!

Sunday was a day of rest. The tavern was closed, though they did take in travelers. By should have enjoyed her respite, but she would rather have been busy. Hard work made time pass faster. Restlessly, she found odd tasks to do.

"Even the Lord rested on the seventh day, By," her mother said when By began polishing pots.

"This needs doing. Besides, working wi' my hands keeps my mind occupied."

"The stables need mucking," Nat said quickly.

"I'm restless, not daft," By replied.

"Light somewhere, Byroney," her father requested. "Your dithering's makin' me tired."

"Tell me a story, By," Nat said, evidently feeling sorry for her. "You haven't told me a tale in ages."

Sighing, she settled in front of the fire. "I'll tell you a tale o' black treachery and bloody murder," she intoned in a somber voice. "In 1692 William III and his wife Mary sat on the throne of England. Scotland was proud, free, and a thorn in the king's side. One especially painful thorn was the powerful Clan MacDonald. King William wished this thorn removed, thinking the other Highland Clans would fall in line could he but do away wi' Laird MacDonald. So, with guile, money, and a black-hearted, greedy traitor, he hatched a plot.

"One blustery February day, when wind whistled down the glens and snow lay upon the peaks of Stob Dearg, a party o' Border Campbell hunters sought refuge at Laird MacDonald's stronghold in Glencoe. Now, the Campbell Clan was no a favorite wi' the MacDonalds, but they were welcomed in accord with Clan law . . ."

"No Scotsman shall ever turn away another Scotsman seeking refuge," Nat said, nodding.

"Aye. Both seeker and giver shall be at peace, old wounds and feuds forgot, when refuge is asked for. So the MacDonalds made the Campbells welcome wi' food, wine, music, and gaming. 'Twas a long and merry evening.

"Then when all had eaten and drunk their fill, they staggered off to bed. The dastardly plot was afoot! The conniving Campbells had only pretended to drink heartily! They waited until all the MacDonalds were fast asleep, then silently crept into the great hall with daggers and swords at the ready.

" 'Who will kill the laird?'

" 'Not I! Not I' chorused these cowards. For Laird MacDonald was known as a fearsome fighter, asleep or no.

"Spying a deck o' cards, the hunt leader whispered, 'We'll draw for it. Whoever draws the jack o' diamonds will have the honor.'

"And so they drew. The man who drew the traitor's card crept up toward the laird's chamber whilst the others fell to murdering their unarmed, sleeping hosts!

"Fortunately, the outcry warned Laird MacDonald, and he jumped from a window, wearing only his nightclothes. He and a few women and bairns lived to tell this tale of treachery.

"When the slaughter was over, blood an inch deep covered the floors o' MacDonald's castle. A great number o' MacDonalds were lost that unholy night. But something else, almost as precious, was lost. The ancient law of hospitality was broken. Trust was broken. The Highlands would never be the same after the massacre at Glencoe."

"No Scot will ever forget that wicked day," her father said mournfully.

"Or the jack o' diamonds," added Nat.

"Aye," Margaret Frazer said, "but it's not just the Campbells who spawn traitors. Jesus had a Judas, if you recall."

"But Judas was no a Scot!" Nat said indignantly.

Ian Frazer laughed. "You're right, laddie. This time 'twas the other way round. A Scot was a Judas. We don't take kindly to that."

"Enough," Margaret said, looking at their glum faces. "Tell us a merry tale, Byroney."

Byroney sighed and complied.

"I brung you a surprise," Nat said, bursting into the cabin late Tuesday afternoon. "Say 'pretty please,' By."

"Pretty please. And shut the door, Nat."

Nat giggled. "Not on your surprise!" He stepped aside, revealing Cam wearing a foolish grin.

"Sorry I don't have no ribbon on me."

"You'll do just fine as you are, Mr. Jones," By said, rushing into his outstretched arms.

"Ma says I hafta practice my readin'," Nat said to anyone who was listening. No one was. "I'll go on upstairs."

According to custom, a courting couple were allowed some private time as long as they weren't totally alone. Over the past year, the Frazers had accepted Cam as By's suitor. His position with Sevier had won him acceptance in the settlement, too.

She led Cam over to the settee by the fire. "Tell me everything."

Cam sighed and held her hand. "Charleston surrendered. Then the Hessians and British sacked the city. It was Godamighty awful, By. Worser'n any Indian raid."

"South Carolina has fallen?"

"Not hardly. The Swamp Fox, Francis Marion, is leading the partisans in quick attacks, dealing hurting blows, then vanishin' afore the English know what hit 'em," he said proudly.

"That's where you've been, isn't it?" Her heart swelled with fear and pride.

"Aye. Jericho and me fit side by side with the South Carolinians. Jericho stopped off at Long Island. I come on here fast as my ole horse could trot."

By swallowed the lump in her throat. "I'm glad you're safe."

"It were touch an' go fer a while there. By the by, I met a friend o' yours," he said. "Will Atwood sends his regards."

"Will? You saw Will? How is he?"

"He was well when I left. Lost most everything when they burnt Charleston, 'cept his wife and chile. They're livin' with some o' her relatives whilst he fights. Purdy good man, yer friend." His emphasis fell slightly on the word friend.

"Will *is* a good friend," she said stoutly. "How'd you meet?"

"We shared a tree. Redcoats had us pinned down fer a long spell. We talked t' pass the time. He's right determined to take Charleston back."

"Do you think we will?"

"General Washington's sent troops and a general named Gates to South Carolina's aid. It's a' lookin' brighter."

"Sometimes I think this war will never end," By said, snuggling closer.

"It will, By. Never fear. I never seed such a scraggly bunch fight so hard and so long fer something."

"War's end can't come too soon for me," she said, straightening as the cabin door burst open.

Colin stuck his head inside. "Cam, hurry over t' the tavern. Colonel Campbell just rode in with news."

"I'm coming, too," By said, grabbing a shawl.

Nat was not far behind.

A fairly large crowd had gathered in the tavern. Colonel Campbell stood on an overturned box to address the group. "I have here a message sent to the Overmountain men from Major Patrick Ferguson of His Royal Majesty's British Army.''

Jeers, hoots, and boos errupted.

"Major Ferguson is annoyed with the help the Overmountain men gave in the Battle of Charleston. He sends word that if we Westerners do not remain quiet in this war, he will march over the mountains, hang our leaders, and lay waste the country with fire and sword.''

The reaction was swift and hot.

"Blighty bastard!''

"Lay us waste? Let him try!''

"Let the bloody Britisher come. We'll be ready!''

Colonel Campbell held up a hand. When the noise quieted, he said, "John Sevier has another notion. I agree. He proposes marching over the mountains and bearding the British lion in his den. How say you?''

The roar of assent shook the rafters.

"Good! I told Sevier I could muster two or three hundred Virginians. If you have a mind to teach that young cub a lesson, sign on with my brother Arthur over here.''

Men surged forward, elbowing for a place in line.

"Sign up and pass the word to your neighbor,'' William Campbell called over the commotion. "We muster a week from today under the Pemberton Oak. We'll join forces with Shelby and Sevier at Sycamore Shoals.''

"We'll larn Patty Fergie a thing or three!''

"Three cheers for the Overmountain men!''

The rafters rang again.

"Oh, I wish I could sign up,'' Byroney exclaimed.

"Well, you can't,'' Nat said, squirming forward. "No girls allowed.''

"No children either,'' By replied, firmly yanking him back by his shirttail. "Here, hold on to him, Ma. I'll have you know I can shoot well as any man, Nathaniel Frazer.''

"Shooting game and shooting men are two different things, Byroney," her father said.

Margaret Frazer held Nat's flailing arms. "Ease off, Nat. I'll need you here. Looks like you'll be the onliest one of my men left to protect me."

"Yer mither's right," Ian said, moving forward in the line.

Somewhat mollified, Nat let himself be dragged behind the bar.

By had her eyes on Cam. She saw him bending to talk with Colonel Campbell, then nod and head for the back door.

She pushed her way out the front and headed for the stables. Cam was already saddling his horse. "Weren't you even going to say good-bye?"

"Knew you saw me leave. Figured you'd come."

"Pretty sure of yourself, aren't you?"

"Nope. Sure o' you," Cam said, smiling. "Like right now. You're fairly bustin' to go and teach ole Fergie a lesson. But seeing the men go off well equipped and satisfied's 'bout all you can do. I know you'll do it well."

Byroney pulled Cam around to face her, threw her arms around his neck, and kissed him soundly. "That'll have to satisfy you till you get back."

"Lordy, By, I hope you don't aim to satisfy all the men that-a-way!" Cam said huskily.

"You go careful, Cameron Jones. Come back to me soon."

"I will. Mayhaps I'll get back afore we ride out, but don't count on it. I got to spread the word far and wide." He leapt upon his horse and rode off.

Preparations for the coming battle went full force. It was a long, hard, two-hundred-mile journey over the mountains into the Carolinas, where they hoped to meet up with Major Ferguson.

Meal was ground for bread making; breads were baked; clothes were sewn; horses were shod and saddles mended. Down on Powder Branch, Mary Patton made three hundred pounds of powder for the militia rifles.

On September 22, 1780, *four* hundred men gathered at the Pemberton Oak, far beyond Colonel Campbell's expectations.

Armed with Deckard and Dillard rifles, tomahawks, and scalping knives, these determined farmers, merchants, teachers, and preachers gathered awaiting the colonel's command to move out.

Byroney, mounted on Liberty, watched her father and two brothers join the ranks. Her heart was near to bursting with pride. The Scottish light of battle danced in her eyes. How she wished to be a man and join this fight!

"Ho, Battle Maid!" cried Evan Kincaid, reining beside her. "You look ready to lead us into the fray."

"Ah, that I could, Evan."

"You must keep the home fires burning for our return."

"I'll do that, for certain. Speaking o' fires, have you gotten the elves out o' your kiln yet?"

"I think I've banished the wee devils. If I can get decent masons come summer, the brickworks will prosper. I still have no woman to fill my grand house though," he said, pulling a sad face.

"You must be blind, Evan Kincaid! The lassies are standing in line for you."

"Ah, but none that I fancy," he said with a mocking smile. He tipped his tricorne and rode off.

A bagpipe skirled on the morning air. In the distance a lone piper turned and marched away.

The massed men followed in straggling formation.

Byroney and all the other well-wishers watched until the last man disappeared over the hill.

Though her eyes ached from looking, Byroney did not see the one tall, rugged figure she wished to see. Where was Cam? Why hadn't he come back? Would he? Was she to spend all her life sitting and waiting?

Sitting was not an option. The absence of three pairs of hands was sorely felt. Already tired from the hectic week of preparation, the Frazers, like most others, worked double time to get in the harvest and take care of normal affairs.

"You look like you been rode hard and put up wet," Peter said late one afternoon.

Byroney stacked the last tray of clean tankards. "Thanks a heap."

"Go grab forty winks whilst there's a lull. Nat's old enough to help out fer a spell."

"I could use a break. Ma should be back from the Nevilles' kraut-making soon."

"Reckon she won't want to eat cabbage for a spell," Peter said, laughing.

"Not even Molly's delicious bubble and squeak! Thanks, Peter." By grabbed her tartan and went out on the porch. The air had an invigorating fallish nip to it already. Maybe she should go over to the north woods and gather some chinquapins. The small nuts made delicious eating on a cold winter night. Grabbing a small basket from the side of the cabin, she strode off.

The mast was heavy this year. Probably meant another hard winter. In no time at all, she had her basket full and turned toward home. Passing her favorite willow, she decided to take a short rest.

The willow provided a snug retreat from the brisk breeze. The creek sang a soothing lullabye. Her back against the knobby trunk, By closed her eyes. . . .

A clip-clop-splash of hooves in water awakened her. Disoriented, she peered into the dusky shadows. Someone was holding a restless horse in the creek! She almost called, "Who's there?" when the distinctive click of a pistol being cocked froze her.

"Who goes there?" a voice hissed.

"It's me, you fool! Put the gun away. Egad! Why did you pick this place?"

A short laugh. " 'Tis not far off the Great Road. You could always say you had to answer a call of nature, if challenged."

"Pah! Are you certain *you* weren't seen?"

"Of course. Did you get your man in place?"

"I did."

"Do you trust him?"

"As much as anyone you can buy. He's my best agent. I arranged two backups in any case."

"Who? I thought this area was a nest of Whigs. What did you tell them?"

"Easy, friend. These two are from Nolichucky, in Sevier's nest of vipers. They're to tally the Overmountain men, then hie off to warn Major Ferguson. There will be no surprise attack."

"And your main man?"

"He's to wait until the line of march is determined and go inform the major. British cannon will be waiting for these partisan upstarts."

"Good. You aren't worried about losing your top agent?"

"Not this fellow. Like a cat, he has nine lives. He'll come out o' this smelling like a rose."

Byroney's heart was pounding so loudly in her ears that she missed the last exchange between the two Tories. Hooves clattering away told her one horseman had departed. Holding her breath, she crept to the edge of the fronds and peered out.

A cloaked figure on horseback was moving cautiously away from her. In the dusk she couldn't see more than an outline! Yet, he was moving toward the Inn!

Slowly, she expelled her held-in air. The militia must be warned! The picture of unsuspecting troops facing waiting British cannon made her blood run cold! It would be a slaughter!

Forgetting her basket, she took off through the woods. Perhaps she could beat the rider to the Inn. Then she could tell everyone what she'd overheard. . . .

Really, Byroney? Will they believe you? Do you have proof? Is this another tall tale, like your ghost Indians? mocked a voice in her head.

"I'll—make—them—listen. Pa would—if he were here." She burst out of the woods. There were no riders on the road! She ran on up toward the Inn. The hitching post was full. Lanternlight and voices spilled from the tavern.

The Frazer cabin was dark.

Hesitating for only a moment, By went toward home. The men had been gone only two days. They were probably still at Sycamore Shoals. She could ride over, tell her pa, and be back by tomorrow sometime. There was a pretty fair road all the way . . .

Without further ado, she went upstairs and changed clothes. Before she left the cabin, she took down Nat's slate and wrote: *Jack o' diamonds, Ma. Must tell Pa. Cover me.* Stuffing her hair under her hat, she sneaked out to the barn.

"Easy, girl," she whispered as her fingers fumbled with Liberty's girth. "We've a long journey this night."

At the last moment, she grabbed Andrew's shepherd's cloak from a peg and wrapped herself in it. It would keep her warm as well as hide any curves that Colin's clothes didn't.

As silently as a thief, rider and horse stole into the night. By prayed she'd remember all the skills Cam had taught her.

Chapter 15

"They're gone already?"

"Left at sunup yesterday," the towheaded boy standing outside the fort replied.

Byroney's weary body crumpled along with her hopes. It had taken all her courage to ride through that last mountain pass—even on a road! "Which way were they headed?"

"Yonder." The boy pointed to lofty mountains looming in the distance.

"Is there a road?"

"Don't rightly know. Ain't never been that fur." He eyed her suspiciously. "You aimin' t' jine 'em?"

Was she? Could she? "I got a message for my Pa," she said, shivering. "Ma don't know where I am. She's gonna skin me alive."

An understanding smile split the boy's face. "Ma wouldn't let me go neither. Reckon how's you could catch 'em if'n you rid hard."

"My horse is tired. Know where I can get another?"

"Naw. Most anythin' worth throwin' a saddle on has been took."

Well, that was it. She couldn't ask more of Liberty than the horse had to give. Casting an apprehensive look at the menacing ring of mountains, she sighed with relief. She wasn't nearly as brave as she'd thought!

Her relief was short-lived. The boy was running an appreciative hand over Liberty. "She be a fine horse. Rest her and oat her and she'll do fer a spell."

Byroney opened her mouth to disagree, but closed it when waiting cannons roared in her mind. "Obliged. Reckon I'll do just that," she heard herself say.

"River's that-a-way. Should still be grazin' 'longside," the boy said, pointing.

Nodding her thanks, By rode off. She was afraid to open her mouth again. Who knew what would come out?

After a short rest and a stretch, she set out. The track of such a large number of men and horses was easy to read. In fact, it was better if she kept her eyes on the trail rather than look at what lay ahead of her.

The farther she went, the worse the weather became. A sleety rain began to fall, its cold damp penetrating her cloak. A shivering mile or so later, she had to move off the trail while two old men driving cattle ambled past.

"Where you headed, son?" one asked.

Deepening her voice, she replied, "Got a message for the militia. You seen 'em?"

The other man laughed. "Us just come from 'em. Us'uns spent the night at Shelving Rock. These hyar beeves was slowin' the march. Me and Lem was sent back with 'em."

"Reckon I could catch up afore nightfall?"

"If'n you can ride th' wind," one scoffed.

"It commenced snowin' up on Roan Mountain. That'll slow 'em up some," the other man said, watching her carefully. "You could cut off some miles was you willin' to go through Devil's Needle. Hit's narrow and slippery, but you'd beat 'em to Yellow Mountain Gap that-a-way, fer sure.''

"Yup. Lem's right. One rider could make it through.''

Leave the trail? The mere thought gave her a belly cramp. She was vigorously shaking her head in refusal when she heard her voice screech, ''Where do I find the Devil's Needle?''

'' 'Bout two miles from here you see a easy-lookin' trail forking left. Hit *is* easy fer 'bout a half mile, then hit gits right troublesome. Onct you thread Devil's Needle you're at the foot o' Yellow Mountain.''

Afraid her voice had given her away, By nodded and rode off before they could ask questions. For the seemingly short two miles, she carried on a furious debate with herself. What was her hurry? She didn't know when the traitors would desert. What if she got lost again? No one would ever know about the traitors or what happened to Byroney Rose Frazer. Why was she doing this foolish thing?

Where the trail branched she reined Liberty. ''Do we challenge the Devil or not?''

Liberty tossed her head and snorted, as if to say, ''It's your decision.''

"I've a strange notion this battle's important, Liberty. We best give it a try.'' Heart thumping wildly, she turned left.

After the temptingly easy part was covered, the faint trail turned out to be more than just ''troublesome''! It switched back upon itself like a writhing snake. Narrow slippery stretches led down into deep gorges, up scree slopes, and between boulders so closely set that Byroney had to dismount and coax Liberty through.

"Old Scratch did himself proud with this place,'' she muttered. To keep her courage up, she quietly sang every tune she knew—several times.

Finally, her cloak in tatters, and both she and Liberty covered in mud and scratches, they emerged from a ravine onto a wider trail.

The trail was chewed by fresh hoofprints!

"Oh wirra! I've missed them!" she wailed and burst into tears. The salty river stung her cuts. She tried to dry her face with her muddy cloak, succeeding only in making matters worse.

Liberty was moving purposefully between some huge boulders beside the trail. Suddenly she dipped her head and began drinking from a small pool.

Hiccuping and sniffling, By dismounted. "Good girl. You found fresh water." She drank from the icy little spring and washed some of the blood and mud from her face. The feeling of utter despair did not wash away.

A strange sound lifted her head and her spirits. Was it marching feet? Hooves? Not trusting her ears, she scrambled atop a boulder.

Coming through the forest was a stream of men and horses!

"Praise God! We didn't miss them!" She hunkered down and scanned the tide of unfamiliar faces. Where were Campbell's men? Her Pa and brothers?

Suddenly, a familiar horse and rider came into view. Byroney jumped up and gave the battle cry of many a Scottish chieftain, "Hie away! To me, Evan!"

Evan's head snapped up. With a startled expression on his face, he fought his way to the boulders. "For God's sake, Byroney, what are you doing out here?" He dismounted and pulled her from her perch. "Why are you dressed in this manner? Do you think you've fooled anyone?"

The spurt of joy she'd felt at seeing Evan vanished. "Let go of me. I have a message for Pa. Where is he?"

Evan shook her roughly. "He isn't here, you little

fool. He's been sent ahead to prepare our night's camp. I can't believe you would do such a foolish thing.''

"It isn't foolish, Evan. It's important to your mission. I need to see Colonel Campbell right away."

Evan still held her shoulders in a punishing grip. "Why? What's this about, Byroney?"

"Unhand her, Kincaid."

Evan spun around.

Byroney darted to one side, afraid her ears had betrayed her.

Cam and Jericho blocked the narrow entrance. A deadly, chilling anger flared in Cam's eyes.

"Cam? . . . Cam, please take me to Pa. I have a message. It's important."

Evan snorted. "Don't be fooled, Jones. Byroney will use any excuse to tag along." He turned to her. "Where are the others, Battle Maid? Couldn't you muster the woman's brigade?"

"It . . . it isn't like that at all," By sputtered.

"Let's hear her out afore we go flingin' words around," Jericho said, putting a restraining arm on Cam. "What brung you here, lass?"

"Traitors! We have traitors amongst us. They're going to warn Ferguson."

"Are these like your ghost Indians?" Evan asked, smiling.

"Shut yer trap, Kincaid, or I'll shut it for you," Cam growled, shaking off Jericho's hand. "Do you have names, By?"

"No. There are two men from Nolichucky in Sevier's party and one amongst Campbell's men," she replied, pouring out her story.

A look passed between Cam and Jericho when she'd finished. "You was right, Jericho," Cam said.

"About what?" asked By.

"We suspicioned two fellers from Nolichucky already," Jericho replied. "They skulked about, ears flappin', anytime a parley took place."

"What about the traitor in our ranks? Any ideas?" Evan asked, now serious.

By rubbed her forehead. "There was something . . . I've thought and thought about it. . . ."

"Don't try too hard, mayhap it'll come," Jericho advised.

"In the meantime, what do we do with Byroney?" Evan asked. "She certainly can't go along with us."

Again, Cam and Jericho exchanged looks.

"Ezra Crockett's?" posed Jericho.

Cam nodded and reached out for Byroney. "Old Ezra will get you back safe. Elk Creek's only a mile or so. You up to it?"

She looked up into his eyes. "I've come this far, another mile or so won't matter." In fact, she'd have ridden another hundred miles to see that gleam of pride in Cam's eyes.

Cam looked at Jericho. "You and Kincaid take her over. I'll see to this."

Jericho nodded. "This hyar'd be a good place to skunk off if they was a' mind to."

Tilting By's face up, Cam brushed his lips against hers. "You done the right thing. Take care."

"You, too."

"If the lovers can part, let's get on with it," Evan said, preparing to mount.

Jericho pulled him back. "We'll let the army pass. No need to cause a stir."

"Whatever you say," Evan replied ungraciously.

Byroney remembered little of their ride to Crockett's. Tiredness enveloped her like a cloak. She did remember Jericho turning her over to a wizened, gnomelike man, and being led into a small, pungent cabin.

"You be safe wi' ole Ez," the man said with a tooth-less smile.

"My horse . . ."

"I'll see t' that beauty. Bed down. We go tomor-row." He gave her a gentle push and she landed on a bearskin-covered pallet. "Ma's gonna kill me." She wasn't sure if she spoke the words or merely thought them.

"Us'll take th' short cut through Elk Creek Pass, Jericho," were the last words she heard before sleep took her.

Chapter 16

"**M**ighty fine breakfast, Mr. Crockett."

"Ezra," he corrected, grinning from ear to ear. "Ain't niver had no 'oman round. Larnt t' do fer myself."

By hid her smile. It was evident this cabin had never known a woman's touch. Clothes, pots, animal traps, and food supplies were scattered with reckless abandon over the snug, one-room cabin. "I'm ready when you are," she said, taking a last swallow of the bitter brew Ezra called mountain tea.

"Horses is ready and waitin'." Without bothering to clear their dishes, Ezra hopped up and grabbed his coonskin cap.

By took the shepherd's cloak from a peg, noting it had been neatly mended whilst she slept. "Much obliged for the repairs, Ezra."

"Gotta keep our gear in prime. Ain't purdy, but hit'll hold."

Liberty wickered a greeting as they came out. She, too, had been brushed, doctored, and fed.

Ezra's mount was a short, fat pony. Even so, he had to hop upon a stump to mount. Cocking his head, Ezra looked her over. "Reckon you done lost yer weapons somewheres."

"I never had any," she confessed, feeling foolish under his gaze. "I didn't plan to be out in the mountains."

"Lord, gel, y'don't step outten yer cabin 'thout being armed!" Quickly, he brushed back his coat, revealing a long knife, pistol, and powder horn. "You best 'member that."

"Yes, sir."

"Keep yer powder dry and one gun loaded alla time. Don't matter none if yer just goin' to the—uh—necessary," he lectured solemnly. "Hit's plumb dangerous out hyar . . . bars, painters, wolves, Injuns, and th' like."

By swallowed hard. She remembered her wild journey yesterday. She'd been lucky. She should have had a weapon. "I'll remember from now on, Ezra."

Satisfied, Ezra nodded and led off.

The trail was faint, like the ones she'd wandered up and down the time she was lost. Ezra, however, traveled quickly—without hesitation. Chattering chickadees, titmice, and finches sang in the oaks, maples, hickories, and ashes. Squirrels skittered, scolding as they passed through the already-multihued carpet of leaves. It was a thoroughly pleasant ride.

By had only one complaint. Ezra, mounted on his pony, was much shorter than she. Sometimes he rode under branches that would have knocked her from the saddle had she not been paying heed. Occasionally, he sang out, "Mind yer head." But mostly he forgot.

They'd been traveling about a half hour when By had to bend almost double again. Just as her cheek touched Liberty's mane, a shot whizzed by.

With a grunt, Ezra toppled from his saddle.

Liberty shied and reared.

By slid to the ground as another shot rang out. Tumbling, she rolled behind a log, almost on top of Ezra. She tried to rise, but he pulled her down.

"Keep . . . low," he wheezed.

"Who's shooting at us? Are you hurt?" Before he answered she saw the bright red stain blossoming on his chest.

"Pistol . . ." he whispered in her ear. "Loaded . . ."

Gingerly, she extracted the gun. Ezra's eyes questioned her. "I can shoot," she answered softly.

"Play . . . possum." Blood frothed between his lips with each word. After one violent shudder, he lay still.

"Oh, wirra! He's dead. This poor, sweet, little man is dead!" Tears sprang to her eyes, blinding her.

The woods were strangely silent. No birds chirped. No squirrels chattered. The only sound was the wind rustling in the treetops.

Possum, she thought, taking small sips of air through her nose. Very slowly, she eased onto her side, pulling her cloak over her right arm. She balanced the hidden pistol over her left arm, let her head droop, and closed her eyes. . . .

Minutes ticked by like years.

Every muscle in her body was screaming before she heard the first twig crack.

Possum . . .

Footsteps . . . moving closer . . . closer . . . closer. . . .

Don't breathe!

Black boots kicked disdainfully at Ezra's body.

Steady . . .

A click of a gun's hammer . . .

Byroney pulled the trigger.

She opened her eyes in time to see the incredulous look on Evan Kincaid's face as he fell backwards, dropping his rifle. The shot whanged harmlessly into the air.

"You . . . shot . . . me!"

"You killed Ezra! Tried to kill me. Why?" By asked, scrambling to her feet and kicking his rifle away. "Why?"

Evan clutched the spurting wound in his belly. His eyes glazed over. Yet a smile curled his paling lips. "Didn't land on my feet this . . . time."

His words hit like a fist. "You? You're the traitor? Why, Evan? Why?"

For a moment the light returned to his eyes. "Money . . . Money and power . . . I will have both . . . no matter who wins this war."

"You have nothing," she said sadly, watching his life ebb away.

With a look of surprise on his face, Evan Kincaid died.

Byroney looked at the two lifeless bodies sprawled on the forest floor and fell to her knees, retching. Traitor or no, she'd killed a person! Tears flooded her cheeks as she rocked back and forth. Her father was right! Killing a person was quite different from killing an animal.

Finally, when there were no tears left, she staggered to her feet. What now? The stench of gunpowder had dispersed on the breeze, but the odor of blood and vomit still cloyed the air. She moved away from the grisly scene. Find Liberty. . . . Find water. . . . Bury Ezra. . . . Evan?

Having a purpose helped. Dazed, she moved down the trail, following the hoofprints. In a clearing a few hundred yards away, she found Liberty and Ezra's pony. Liberty came to her easily, but it took some minutes to catch the pony.

It was worth the effort. Ezra had a water bottle slung on his saddle. By rinsed her mouth several times before swallowing. Nothing seemed to remove the horrid, bitter taste. Spying a gnarled sassafras tree, she broke off a twig and chewed. It helped some.

A sense of urgency filled her, but she couldn't seem to move very fast. Her feet felt as if she were wading through deep, cold water. Leading both animals and shivering, she reluctantly retraced her steps.

Without warning, Liberty snorted and tossed her head, almost ripping the reins from Byroney's hand.

Clutching the reins tightly, By stood dead still. The hairs on her neck rose. An eerie feeling that she was not alone swept over her. Eyes darting and barely breathing, she scanned the woods. Nothing moved. . . .

"Byroney."

Her name in that soft, familiar whisper . . . She whipped her head around just as Cam stepped from behind an oak. For a moment she thought she was dreaming . . . making Cam appear out of her desperate need. . . .

Cam moved toward her. "Are you wounded?"

Dropping the reins, she ran into his outstretched arms. "Oh, Cam, Ezra's dead . . . Evan Kincaid shot him . . . *I* shot Evan . . . Shot him dead. . . ."

Cam held her tightly until she stopped babbling and shaking.

Finally, By pulled away from the comfort of his arms. "Why are you here? How did you find me?"

"Kincaid slipped outta camp last night. When I come back from taking care o' those two from Nolichucky, Jericho was afixing to take out after Kincaid. Jericho was more'n a little suspicious o' him after some o' the tales he told on you. I hightailed it to Ezra's, but you'd already left. I followed and heard the gunshots. When I come upon where you was bushwhacked it nearly scairt me t' death! Thought I'd find you dead some-wheres along th' trail." He tightened his grip on her shoulders as they walked.

"I would have been if Ezra hadn't given me his pistol and told me how to use it," she said, shivering again. "I'm glad you and Jericho were suspicious. I never was. I might have put things together and come up with Evan as the traitor, but I misdoubt it."

"Kincaid thought you would. He planned to shut your mouth forever."

"I know." She swallowed hard. "What do we do now?"

"I bury the dead and take you home," Cam answered firmly.

"You'll miss the battle!"

"There'll be others. I learnt me something today, Byroney. Freedom won't mean much to me lest I have you by my side. I aim to speak to your Pa soon as it's fittin'."

"For true, Cam?"

"For true, Byroney Rose. I'll change my name, run, or do whatsomever it takes t' have a life with you." He sealed his pledge with a kiss that shook her to her very foundation.

When they broke apart, she said, "I've learned something, too. I'm an ardent Patriot, but I don't want to be a soldier."

Cam chuckled. "Want or not, you are. The success o' this battle hangs partly on surprise. We'll be outnumbered and outgunned. You give us a chance."

"You won't be outfought!" she replied, not missing the longing in his voice.

"Nope, I allow that t' be Major Ferguson's second surprise."

Byroney was thinking hard. "Cam, did you tell anyone about me?"

"No. Didn't have time."

"How about Jericho?"

Cam frowned. "Don't think he'd say nothing till I returned. Be demoralizin' on the men. Why?"

A tale was taking shape in her head. "Then don't tell anyone, Cam."

"Why not?"

"I'd just as soon not give folks more to jaw about," she hedged.

They had reached the ambush site. Cam turned to block her view, eyeing her suspiciously. A frown of disapproval uglied his rugged face. "Your ma knows where you're at, don't she?"

"More or less," By said, talking quickly. "I left her a coded message: 'Jack o' diamonds. Must warn Pa. Cover me.' She will, too. So nobody at Wolf Hills will know where I've been or why. I'll tell Pa when he gets home."

Cam was bewildered by her spate. "Jack o' diamonds? What's playin' cards got t' do with this?"

By slowed her rush of words. "Jack o' diamonds is the traitor's card in Scotland. It's a long, dreary story, Cam. I'll tell you all o' it some other time. But I used it to keep any Tories from knowing we were onto them. They could have made other plans."

"Reckon that makes sense."

"Yes, but it will be for naught if you come riding in with me! Folks will know something's amiss for you to miss this fight. So you set me on the right trail and go on back like you just been out scouting. It'll outfox any Tory plans."

"Send you back alone?"

"I got here by myself! If you get me to Devil's Needle, I'll get home," she declared with every ounce of conviction she could muster. She stood straight as an arrow and stared him down . . . not missing the gleam of hope in his eyes.

Suddenly, Cam laughed. " 'Tis no wonder I love

you, Byroney Rose. You have the cunning of a fox and the spirit of a' eagle.''

''You'll do it then?''

Cam nodded. '' 'Tis a good plan. You go up yonder t' that big oak and turn right. You'll find Kincaid's horse tied up a little ways down. We'll pack these two out an' I'll bury 'em later.''

Twenty minutes later Cam had completed the first part of his grisly task. ''Let's be away.''

By sent up a silent prayer for both men, though Evan would need it more, she thought.

At the boulders where only yesterday she'd hailed Evan, she and Cam dismounted. Cam filled Ezra's canteen at the spring and handed it to her. He'd already insisted she carry Ezra's knife, pistol, and bedroll. ''If you go steady, you should reach Sycamore Shoals afore nightfall. Someone'll put you up for th' night. You stay, you hear me?''

By tossed her head. ''Don't be so persnickity. We aren't married yet, Cam Jones!''

For an answer, Cam crushed her to him and kissed her until her head swam. ''Speakin' o' marryin', you think we could do that right soon?'' he asked huskily.

''Around Christmas suit you?''

''If that's soon as you can make it, I'm willin'.''

By laughed and swung into the saddle while her legs still had the strength. ''Whip the British and come back to me soon, Cam.''

''I'll do both, God willin'. Ride wary, luv.''

''You, too.'' With a wave, she guided Liberty into the Devil's Needle.

Two days later—knife and pistol now hidden in her bedroll—she rode up to Wolf Hills Inn.

Her mother rushed out of the cabin. ''Byroney, you're back. How is Charity?'' she called.

''Better, Ma. We had a good visit.''

Nat came running from the tavern room. "I'll put up your horse, By."

"Much obliged. Give her a double ration o' oats. She's been a bonny lass."

"Come tell me the news," her mother said, beckoning.

The Inn had emptied with all the shouting. "We're next," one of the regulars said. "We've missed your singing and harp-playing, Byroney."

"I'll be over directly. Let me gossip with Ma first."

It was quite a little while before Byroney honored her word and went to the Inn.

Epilogue

On October 7, 1780, the Overmountain men defeated Major Patrick Ferguson's army at the Battle of Kings Mountain. Major Ferguson and 120 of his men died in the surprise attack.

Only forty Patriots fell. Having done what they set out to do, the Overmountain men marched home to harvest their crops, prepare for winter, and take care of their families. Citizen soldiers, one and all.

On December 15, 1780, Byroney Rose Frazer wed Cameron Jones in the Presbyterian Church.

Afterward, Ian Frazer threw the grandest Scottish ceilidh ever seen on the frontier. Music, laughter, and dancing people filled Wolf Hills Inn to overflowing.

"I cain't believe you're finally my wife—Miz Cameron Jones," Cam said, holding By's hands.

"Oh, but I am!"

"Aye," Ian Frazer said, sweeping Byroney away in his arms and into the dance. "You have a bonny new name now, my wee lass. But whatever the name, you'll always be the innkeeper's daughter."

"That I will, Pa. The innkeeper's daughter I'll always be."

*   *   *

Years later, Thomas Jefferson would write that the Battle of Kings Mountain was the turning point in the War for Independence.

Few people ever knew of the part played by the innkeeper's daughter. That was quite all right for Byroney Jones. She and Cam were happily conquering other frontiers.

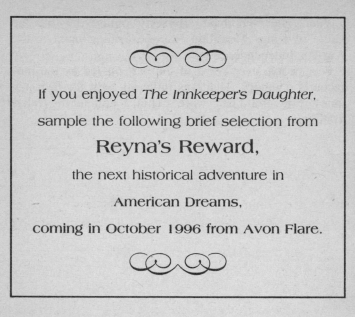

If you enjoyed *The Innkeeper's Daughter*,

sample the following brief selection from

Reyna's Reward,

the next historical adventure in

American Dreams,

coming in October 1996 from Avon Flare.

Spring, 1814
The Gulf of Mexico

Reyna Maria Alvaron cowered in the darkest corner of the ship's cabin, cringing every time she heard a new scream of pain or a bloodcurdling yell. Even with her hands covering her ears, she could hear the muffled sounds of battle overhead.

The sharp clang of metal upon metal rang out as saber met cutlass. She heard crashes, bumps, and thumps; the splash of objects being thrown overboard. The ship shuddered at every cannon blast. Smoke singed the air.

Sister Augustine bravely faced the bolted door, a heavy flintlock pistol clutched in both shaking hands. The Spanish captain had loaded it before he left to join the battle. One lead ball stood between them and unknown agony, and it was anybody's guess whether the good Sister could pull the trigger anyway.

The pirate ship had stalked them through the morning fog, the captain said, coming up out of the burned-off mist too fast and too close to outrun. Cutthroats were now on board, and Reyna wondered how the Spanish crew would fare against them.

"They're coming, *querida*," whispered Sister Augustine. The feisty nun planted her feet in a firm stance and braced her shoulders against the wooden pillar that supported the ceiling of their simple quarters. They had shared this cabin almost twenty-four hours a day for five weeks during the slow, often storm-tossed voyage from Spain.

The door handle rattled. Curses rang out. A heavy object crashed against the portal, time and time again, until the wood splintered and the pirates broke through. The room seemed to vibrate. Reyna crouched farther back in her hiding place, and peeked around the corner.

A deeply tanned pirate, with an unkempt beard and a bandanna covering his head, burst into the tiny room. Several ruffians stood guard at the entryway. They leered at the frightened nun as the gun wavered in her hands.

"Ah! Holy One!" the swarthy sailor said. "What are you doing with a weapon? Surely, you would betray your sacred vows if you were to shoot me dead." His laughter chilled Reyna as thoroughly as had the icy wind sweeping across the Atlantic.

"Why are you aboard this puny vessel?" The pirate jerked the gun out of Sister's grasp.

Defenseless and outraged, she stood her ground. "Do not advance one step farther, young man. Even you could not stand against God's wrath if you were to harm me." Her voice wavered, but she held her head high so that she could look down her nose at the blustering pirate.

"Holy Mary, Mother of God, I would not harm nary a hair on your head—if hair be growing there. Come now. Let us leave this airless pit. Come topside and meet my captain."

The good Sister signaled from behind her skirts for Reyna to remain hidden. The grizzled sailor escorted the nun out of the cabin, but the girl fully expected the raiders to turn around and come back for her.

Fresh air slowly filtered into the tiny cabin from the open door, and Reyna began to breathe again. She was sure she had held her breath for the last ten minutes. Compared to moments before, the ship now seemed to be sitting still on an ocean of glass.

A deafening silence replaced the battle noise.

She waited what seemed an eternity, lulled by the splish-splash of water against the wooden hull and the cry of a lone gull riding the wind. Surely she had not been abandoned. Surely Sister Augustine would not leave her here to die . . . unless death was a better fate than what lay ahead with the pirates . . . or, Heaven forbid, the good Sister had already met her own end at the hands of those wicked men.

Reyna slowly crept to the door, listened, then padded on bare feet to the ship's ladder that led topside. Once she climbed the steep steps, she would be immediately exposed, but Reyna had lost all patience for cringing below in fear. *It is better to face what lies ahead than to skulk in the shadows.*

Reyna started up the ladder. She glimpsed above her the ripple of white sails against a blue-gray sky. Suddenly it seemed critical that she gain the deck and be unconfined.

When her head cleared the hold, she was revived by

a deep breath of clean salt air. But then a man's steely voice, with the hint of a French accent, startled her from behind.

"Ah, my little beauty," he said pleasantly. "We've been wondering when you would appear."

Historical Adventure and Romance with the AMERICAN DREAMS Series from Avon Flare

SARAH ON HER OWN
by Karen M. Coombs   78275-8/$3.99 US/$5.50 Can
When she leaves England to sail to the New World, love is the last thing Sarah expects to find.

PLAINSONG FOR CAITLIN
by Elizabeth M. Rees   78216-2/$3.99 US/$5.50 Can
Caitlin's heart belonged to the American West . . . and the man who taught her to love it.

INTO THE WIND
by Jean Ferris   78198-0/$3.99 US/$5.50 Can
Nowhere in her dreams did Rosie imagine sailing the high seas on a pirate ship!

SONG OF THE SEA
by Jean Ferris   78199-9/$3.99 US/$5.50 Can
Together Rosie and Raider challenge the dangers of uncharted waters and unfulfilled dreams.

WEATHER THE STORM
by Jean Ferris   78198-0/$3.99 US/$4.99 Can
Fate conspired to keep Rosie and Raider apart, yet their love was even more powerful.